Forty Acres and Maybe a Mule

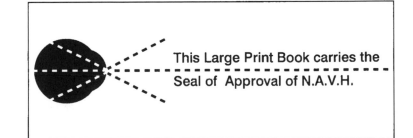

This Large Print Book carries the
Seal of Approval of N.A.V.H.

Harriette Gillem Robinet

Forty Acres and Maybe a Mule

Thorndike Press • Thorndike, Maine

This book is dedicated to our grandchildren,
present and future. We love you:
Alison Nicole Hall, Michael Steven Hall,
Conrad David Schillinger-Robinet, and
Kaitlin Christine Hall.

Chapter One

Pascal hadn't been able to fall asleep that night. Around the plantation the air seemed full of whispered secrets. As he lay in the cabin doorway, he worried about how people treated him now that Mama was dead.

After work that afternoon he had walked past some men and said, "How y'all doing?" They had stopped talking. Didn't they know that, even though he worked in the Big House, he wouldn't tell the master?

In fact, he had secretly saved one of those men from a beating one day. Master had seen the slave with apples he had picked to feed his children. As soon as Master had run after the man, Pascal had used his big walking stick to break a window. When Master turned back to run to his Big House, the other slave and Pascal had both escaped.

That had been last fall. It was now spring, and Pascal wanted to know the secrets folks were buzzing about. He bet the news had something to do with the War Between the States.

The night air by his slave cabin door was spring-blossom sweet, but that April of 1865 it seemed full of mystery besides. He listened to the breathing of six other slaves who lay with him on the crowded cabin's dirt floor. From his pad, he glanced out the open doorway.

In the black South Carolina sky a half-moon mothered a million dancing stars. The night sky comforted Pascal's hurt feelings. Soon he felt some of the peace and joy that Mama always had talked about.

When a shadow hesitated by his doorway, Pascal sat up. "Who's that?" he asked in a whisper.

"Pascal? It's me, Gideon."

"Gideon? You be back? Be that really you, Gideon?" Pascal could hardly believe it. His heart seemed squeezed-to-bursting with happiness. As he stood to hug his tall brother, tears flowed from his eyes. How wonderful to have his brother back! Gideon had run away from the plantation two years ago. And he hadn't gotten caught or killed in the war, as everyone had thought.

"Yes, it be me all right. I came back for you and Mama."

"Gideon" — Pascal trembled — "Mama ain't here."

Tall, wiry Gideon glanced down the row of two dozen slave cabins. "Where's Jerusalem City? Where she be? I be leaving tonight. Don't want no trouble with Master."

"Mama's dead, Gideon. She kept asking for more food for the slaves. Folks saw the overseer shoot her down by the creek."

Every time he thought about Mama getting shot, Pascal felt a fist ball up in his stomach. That white man just murdered his mama. How Pascal missed her; since then he had felt lost. Seemed like Mama just up and left him to the mercy of the world.

Since her death, he hadn't had any family left among the slaves. With Mama and Papa dead, and with Gideon gone and four other brothers sold years ago, Pascal had been alone. Before she died, Mama had told him news; and she had given him something to look forward to, even if it was just a buttered biscuit left on the master's plate. Afterward, there was no one to care.

But now Gideon was back.

Gideon pulled Pascal to his side, hugged him, and rested his chin on his little brother's head. Pascal felt warm, close to his brother. No one had hugged him since Mama died.

Gideon heaved a sigh and said, "All this time I wanted to tell Mama. I wanted to tell her so bad. You know we be free now?"

"Free?" Pascal held his breath and wiped his eyes. Was this the news the other slaves were whispering about? "Walls of Jericho! You sure now, Gideon?"

"Sure we free," said a voice from Pascal's cabin. "But Master ain't letting none of us go, nor paying us to work, neither."

Another voice said, "And them that go just walk a little ways down the lane and come back. Some proud darkies keep walking and starve. I don't wanna starve."

"Freedom?" asked another voice. "There ain't no white folks what gonna let us live free! What's freedom mean for colored folks in South Carolina?"

Gideon shouted, "Freedom means everything!"

Pascal's heart began to pound faster. Freedom did mean everything.

"Hush you now," said a woman. "Don't be getting us in trouble, Gideon. Master angry about this freedom talk and he might come walking down this way tonight."

"But it ain't just talk," said Gideon. "President Lincoln freed us slaves two years ago. And better still, now we gonna have our own land."

"Land?" Men from other cabins scrambled to crowd around Gideon. They called, "Hey, y'all, Gideon's back and he say we can own land."

Pascal nodded. With land they really could be free!

Dressing quickly, he stuffed all he owned — shirt, tin cup, hairbrush, and three marbles — into a potato sack. He tied the sack on his walking stick and limped to the door. They could own land to farm? Now there was something to look forward to!

Pascal was so excited he almost tripped over his lame foot. Where had Gideon been all this time? How far had he traveled? Questions exploded in his mind, but he would wait to ask them. People were whispering and chuckling in a circle around Gideon.

"Already happening," Gideon said.

As Pascal walked away, he heard, "General Sherman already gave land to some of us who done followed him through the South. Forty acres and maybe a mule's just for the asking for colored people, like homesteading been for white people."

Pascal heard slaves stirring and talking in the cabins he passed. "Who's that down the row?" a woman asked.

"Gideon's back," a man told her. "Say

they giving out forty acres and maybe a mule to slaves."

The woman snorted. "Gideon always been a sound-off. Worried Jerusalem City 'cause he never took kindly to slavery. It be a wonder he's alive."

"That woman be a sound-off herself," another woman said, "sassing the overseer. She got herself shot dead."

"Yeah, but Missus gave us more food, didn't she?"

Heart drumming, Pascal ran stumbling along the path. From birth his weak right leg was bent inward at the knee, and that leg was shorter. His right hand was weak, too. He reached the cabin he wanted at last. "Nelly," he whispered through the doorway.

"That you, Pascal? What be going on?" She stepped out.

"My brother Gideon's here. Say we free and can own land now. I be going with him, my own brother. You wanna come?" He took a deep breath. "Come on, Nelly." Pascal had protected Nelly ever since the master had bought her a year ago. Nelly had biscuit-tan skin color and full moon eyes of honey brown.

For two years they had been free, but the masters were still selling and buying slaves. Pascal wondered at that.

Twisting a braid, Nelly said, "You be like my brother."

Pascal squeezed her hand. "You're right. We be family. So, come on, Nelly. It's true. Gideon say we been free for two years. Free!"

She said, "Master won't let none of us go."

"Gideon's here. We be running away with him."

Nelly twisted another one of her braids.

"Your mama be dead," he said. "What's to keep you? You got no family here. Besides, if you stay after I run away, Master gonna treat you something awful at the Big House."

Once, a hidden Pascal had used his stick and tripped Master when he was drunk, to keep him from kicking Nelly. Nelly had run, and Master never found out why he fell and got that cut lip.

At first Nelly stared at Pascal. Then in seconds she dressed, tied clothes in a shawl, and followed him.

When Pascal returned, Gideon asked, "You ready?" Then he noticed Nelly. Pascal was about twelve, but Nelly was only about eight years old. Like Pascal, she was thin. She wore her hair in six long braids. Twisting one of them, she stared at Gideon. Since she was new at the plantation, she had never seen him before.

"Who she be?" asked Gideon as he looked her up and down.

"My friend Nelly. She be coming with us, Gideon."

Gideon tapped his army boot. "I hope she ain't gonna slow me down none," he said. Glancing at Pascal, he shook his head. "No more than you, lame leg."

Pascal flinched. Gideon could be mean sometimes.

"Take them, Gideon," called a woman from the cabin. "Master find new children to shoo the flies off his plate. They ain't worth nothing."

Head down, Pascal felt as if he had been slapped. Folks didn't think much of him or of Nelly, but things were gonna change. They were gonna find land and be owners. Then he would have a family and a family farm, too. He straightened his shoulders and raised his head.

Gideon waved at the people standing around him in the moonlight. "You people stay here in the slimy shame of slavery. You nobodies! I be free and on my way to own land. Landowners are somebody!" He laughed.

Folks stepped back.

Pascal stared at his brother. What he said might have stung some folks, but the words *landowners are somebody* sounded fine.

Without another word, Gideon strode away in the dark, stooping under low tree branches. Waving goodbye, Pascal and Nelly followed. She stopped for a small cooking pot and a tin cup, then they ran to catch up. Already they had lost Gideon.

Mosquitoes buzzed. Their bites stung Pascal's arms and legs. As the two children scrambled uphill along the path, cicadas and crickets sang everywhere. Pascal's heart fluttered as if he were a canary let out of a cage.

Chapter Two

Nelly and Pascal pushed past trees and through scratchy brush.

"Pascal, are we lost?" Nelly asked.

"No, Nelly," he said, "we be up to the road soon."

"When we get there, how we gonna know which way to go? I be scared, Pascal. Master gonna catch us."

Pascal took her hand in his weak, twisted one. He was frightened, too, but he had to be brave. "It's just that Gideon's impatient," Pascal said. "He be coming back for us soon."

Pascal thought back. Mama had tried to keep Gideon out of trouble. He sometimes stuck a burr under a saddle to make a horse throw the overseer, but one day he was caught. And he had planned days when the young slaves all slowed down in the field. Sometimes he got blamed for that, too. He

16

got whipped all the time, but he kept on until Master grew angry and found a buyer. When Gideon found out that he had been sold, he ran away. They hadn't heard from him, and Mama had wondered if he was still alive.

Mama had had six children, all boys: four of them sold away, Gideon, who ran, and Pascal, who was the youngest. He couldn't even remember his older brothers' names, let alone know where they were.

Should he have followed Gideon? Yes, Pascal decided. Gideon needed Pascal, and he, Pascal, needed Gideon. They were family. Nelly, too. And nothing was more important than family.

Pascal sighed and said, "Just think, Nelly, we won't be running errands, fanning breezes, and shooing flies for Master no more. We free children now." He had to distract her.

She nodded. "No more whippings at the whipping tree." She squeezed his hand. "I hope."

To make her feel better as they climbed, he practiced animal sounds. He imitated an owl. "What's that?"

"Screech owl," she whispered.

He chattered in a high voice. "What's that?"

"Squirrel. You a regular woodland all by yourself, Pascal."

"And this?" He stopped, made a call, and grunted.

"A deer?" As she spoke, a fawn stepped out of the bushes, looked at them with large, innocent eyes, and scampered away. Pascal was thrilled; he really did make good animal imitations.

He asked, "You know what a moose call his wife?"

"No."

"Deer." They both giggled and walked on.

When they climbed out of the bushes onto a dirt road, Pascal stared up and down. Where was Gideon? Had he left them? Pascal felt sick to his stomach.

Nelly pointed. "I be hearing voices that way."

As they ran, Pascal stayed close to the grassy ditch along the roadside and kept Nelly with him, both ready to hide in the ditch. He carried his stick in his strong hand. Around a bend, he saw Gideon talking to a colored soldier. That seemed safe. Pascal and Nelly ran up.

"Where you been?" asked Gideon, laughing at them.

Pascal didn't answer. He felt blood rush to his face, and his heart was pounding.

Gideon was good-hearted, but he didn't always act that way. Mama said slavery had set a fire of anger deep inside Gideon.

The soldier slapped Gideon's back. "Of course I seen you. Can't miss a tall, thin African like you. Didn't you follow General Sherman from Atlanta to Savannah?"

"Yes, sir," said Gideon. "I dug latrines and graves. This cap I got be off a dead soldier. The boots, too."

"The war's 'most over," said the soldier. "I finished duty, and be on my way home. I hope you find a place to farm, son."

Gideon said, "I hope you find your family well."

He turned to Pascal and Nelly. "Come on. First we gotta escape Master." He shook his head sadly. "Lordy, but I miss Mama. I was so looking forward to seeing Mama."

Knapsack and folding shovel on his back, Gideon took them each by a hand. They had to run to keep up with his long-legged strides. "Now this the way it be," he said. "At every town big enough, while you two hide in the woods, I gonna ask if they got a Freedmen's Bureau. We want land in South Carolina."

"Can't we ask with you?" Pascal said. Freedmen's Bureau. *Freedmen!* What a beautiful word, he thought.

19

For a few moments, Gideon didn't speak. "You take care of Nelly here," he said. "Just in case some white man get mad. I'll do the finding out."

Across Gideon, Pascal glanced at Nelly. She looked as frightened as he felt. One after another, Nelly was twisting her braids. Pascal knew he could be brave, but at the same time he was terrified. Was it safe to go with Gideon? What kind of freedom was this?

Pascal had always thought freedom would be like Joshua and the walls of Jericho in the Bible. Inside the walls of slavery they were bought, sold, separated from family, whipped, kept hungry, and sometimes worked to death. But God would raise up Joshua to blow a horn; and colored people would all shout. And those walls would come tumbling down forever. That would be freedom!

Gideon went on. "This place called Freedmen's Bureau be where they giving out land to men with families."

Pascal frowned. "You ain't a man and you ain't got a wife," he said.

Gideon jerked Pascal's hand. "Ain't nobody saying I ain't a man when I sign up for my forty acres. If I ain't old enough, I'm tall enough." Nelly gazed up at him and nodded.

Pascal sighed. The way he figured, he himself was twelve or maybe thirteen years old — he didn't know his springtime birth month exactly — and that meant Gideon was only about sixteen or seventeen; but Gideon was tall. Maybe they could get that family farm after all!

For the first week of escaping, they traveled the roads by night and rested hidden in the woods by day. Pascal's feet were soon bleeding from stones in the roads. Leaning on his stick made his good hand sore; and he was sleepy day and night. Sometimes his eyes were closed, and he let Gideon drag him along. Nelly moaned in her sleep. She must have been tired as well, but she never admitted it. Gideon had money for bread and cabbage; they drank from creeks and ditches.

The first time Gideon went into town and then returned to the woods, Pascal asked, "What'd they say? Can we get our forty acres here?"

"No," said Gideon. "Man said he don't know 'bout no freedom for slaves. He say go back and plant the master's fields. But his white face say it be a red-face lie."

Nelly shrugged. "I don't much like it 'round here noways. Too close to Master."

"Next place gonna be better," Pascal said, nodding.

At the next stop, Pascal asked the same question.

"No," his brother said, "they say we crazy to be thinking slaves could be smart enough to farm land. Say, 'Go back.'"

At the next town, Nelly asked, "What they say, Gideon? Do they got our land?"

"No, man wanna know who told me. I said General Sherman, and the man cussed and shook his fist."

The next time Gideon returned, Pascal asked, but Gideon didn't answer. His cheek was swollen, and the skin under his eye grew purple. That evening Nelly held a cool rag, wet at the ditch, on his face.

In the second week, since they were farther from Master, they walked in daylight. It was easier for Pascal to sleep at night and stay awake in the daytime.

"Pascal," Nelly said one morning as they sat eating, "I used to dread growing up. Wasn't nothing pleasant to look forward to. Now I feel different." She sipped water.

"After the overseer shot Mama dead, I felt dead, too," said Pascal. "My own wonderful mama, and I couldn't save her. It was hard to believe at first. I felt helpless, empty in my heart. After a while I was sad, then I began

feeling mad at her for getting herself killed."
He chewed a crust of bread.

"I got sold right after my mama died giving birth. I hardly ever saw her and I don't know what happened to the baby." Nelly sighed. "Different old aunties raised me, but I wanted my own mama. I be so thin, I think First Master thought I was gonna die, too, so he sold me. But now we be free children. What you reckon owning land be like?"

Pascal stretched out on the ground and put his hand behind his head. "We'll wake up singing and go to bed laughing," he said. "Mama used to say joy was peace dancing, and peace was joy resting. We be having both joy and peace."

Gideon glanced over. "The green grasshoppers gonna call, 'Yassa, boss,'" he said, "and the white daisies will bow down as we colored landowners strut past."

Nelly giggled. "I still can't believe it."

"Believe it," said Gideon, tearing off bread. "Slavery been an embarrassment to the white man, that's what them Union soldiers told me. Now things gonna be different. We got a right to be free, that's what I learned from soldiers. And I learned reading and writing. Big Irishman taught me for two years. He caught a shot in the

23

chest." Gideon covered his face with both hands.

"As he died," Gideon said in a muffled voice, "I rocked that white man in my arms like a baby. Me and some others dug his grave." He patted his shovel. "Now, thanks to him, I be ready for freedom. We may have to go all the way to Georgia. Maybe they be having a Freedmen's Bureau there."

Little by little Pascal was learning what his brother had been doing those two years. Gideon stood, and they started walking for the day.

A colored man and woman walked up to them. "Please, can you spare some food? We ain't eaten for two days." Gideon, always generous, gave them bread.

Farther along the road a group of colored men called, "Y'all hear of anywhere they hiring for pay?"

"No," said Gideon, "but I think they giving out land in Georgia."

In spite of the disappointments, the farther he walked from the master's plantation, the freer Pascal felt. The trip was like a holiday. On the roads were hundreds of soldiers going home after battles, and hundreds of freed slaves looking for a better life. The lanes were almost crowded. Since Pascal had seldom left his master's plantation before, this was exciting.

Pascal knew the freed folks all wanted a better life, but he also knew it took courage to look for it after being slaves all their lives.

White people had called slaves dumb and lazy, but most slaves knew better. Pascal worked at the Big House and knew how many dumb things white people did. And slaves were always outsmarting the master about egg laying, tools breaking, and pig births. Not even the overseer knew what happened in the fields. Yet even so, it could be scary for slaves to run away to freedom.

Each small farm Pascal passed gave him hope that one day they would have a little family farm, too. Now he had a family and a future. He promised himself to fight to keep them.

As they walked, Pascal saw several lanes leading to plantations where curtains flapped sadly in broken windows at the Big House. At one mansion a cannonball had torn off half the roof. White children peeked from an open room.

Pascal looked at them and said to Nelly, "Southern white folks be plenty angry at the North. President Lincoln's trying, but this freedom ain't gonna be that easy."

A man walked up. "Please, y'all know my daughter Miranda Smith? She cook for the masters?" The man held his hat across his chest. "She was sold five years ago."

"No, sir," Pascal told him. Gideon offered him bread.

"Gideon," said Pascal, "I been looking at folks. You know, we got four brothers what were sold to masters out there somewhere."

Gideon grunted. "I found one. Talked to him just before he died. Came upon a man looked like Mama, but he was light in skin color, you know. I asked him if he came from South Carolina, and he said he was sold from there as a boy. When he said his mama be Jerusalem City, I knew he be our brother. When I told him I be Gideon, his baby brother, he smiled and died."

"Really?" asked Pascal. "What he be like?"

"Tall and thin, light. Name of Galilee. Looked like Mama's nose and smile." Gideon shook his head. "By the time I knew he be my brother, he was near dead. I buried him."

"Tell me more," begged Pascal.

"That be all to tell."

"What about the others? Do you remember their names?"

"Not rightly."

One brother dead. Pascal turned and

stared at a man on the road. Was this man his lost brother?

He cleared his throat. So much suffering; people were hungry at heart, and hungry in body. He thought about the twelve slaves on their plantation who had starved last winter. That's why Mama had asked for more food.

Pascal shivered.

Chapter Three

By the end of the second week, men in nine towns had told Gideon to go back to his master. No place seemed to have a Freedmen's Bureau; or if it did, no one would admit it.

The sun shone brightly as Pascal and Nelly walked along the road one day. Pascal thought those nine towns had been too close to the master's plantation. Going farther seemed safer. He still felt hopeful.

"Look," Nelly said, "see if you can make your shadow dance." She held out her skirt and swayed.

The sun gave them skinny shadows, but sometimes their shadows grew fat on roadside grass. Watching shadows made the walking fun; and although he was tired and fearful, at the same time Pascal's heart sang for joy. He felt that somewhere a Freedmen's Bureau waited for them. They were on their way to the promised land!

Soon Gideon pointed to a wooded hillside for that evening's rest. "We been walking two weeks and we near Georgia now," he said. "A man at that last store said it be only a few miles more. Maybe South Carolina ain't got no Freedmen's Bureau yet. Georgia got them, I hope. That be where General Sherman been giving out land. I can hardly wait to work my own land, grow my own crops. Forty acres and maybe a mule!"

"You reckon boll weevils gonna get in our cotton?" asked Nelly. A crew of weevils, each the size of half her smallest fingernail, could ruin a cotton crop. She stood staring at him.

"They dare not," Pascal said. He raised his stick.

"Any boll weevils in my cotton gonna get whipped at the tree," Gideon said. "I'll show them who be the boss of my land!"

Nelly giggled. "Get on, Gideon. Suppose it don't rain none?" She looked at Pascal, who rubbed his chin.

"Rain for my crops?" Gideon asked. "Ain't you never heard about 'taste and see the goodness of the Lord'? We gonna have rain every midnight, no puddles by dawn, and cotton will rise up by noon singing hallelujah!"

Nelly sighed. "Will we have good victuals to eat?"

Gideon nodded. "Gonna eat high up on the hog. No more pig's feet, and pig's ears, and pig's tails. We am eating pork chops and hams, greens swimming in pot juice, and rice so fluffy white it look like clouds out of heaven."

Pascal's stomach was so empty that he felt dizzy. He swallowed. "Biscuits every Sunday?" he asked, dropping his sack.

"Biscuits dripping with butter every day," Gideon said. "We ain't just saving them for Sunday like white folks do. We colored folks gonna celebrate every day beginning soon's we can."

Pascal, leaning on his stick, asked, "Listen, ain't that a carriage coming?"

Nelly ran to a leafy tree and climbed up the trunk to hide. Pascal threw their sacks behind bushes and hid in some brush with Gideon behind him. He heard the clip-clop of the horse and the creaking of the wagon wheels. From his hideout Pascal watched.

In the distance colored people ran into the woods, all but one. The wagon would pass an old colored man limping down the road. This gentleman had been behind them for miles. The wagon was a small, two-wheel carriage with a well-dressed young white man driving. He called, "Hello there, uncle," and slowed the horse to a stop.

The old man removed his battered straw hat. "Hello, sir. Don't call me uncle. Call me Mister Freedman."

Freedman. So the old man had taken that beautiful name. Pascal smiled. Maybe they needed a freedom name.

With a curse the young man raised his whip to threaten the old man, but the old gentleman stood as straight as he could. Shaking the reins, the young man cursed again.

Pascal's spastic arm jerked on his chest. Holding his arm down, he backed farther into the bushes and hugged his stick close. He clenched his jaw until it hurt. How dare that white man curse this gentleman!

"You lazy Negroes are wandering the roads instead of getting our farms ready for planting. Where you been, uncle?"

The old man looked down now. "Young sir, I searched for my wife 'cause Master sold her. I found where she used to work and saw where she be buried dead."

"Who owns you, uncle?"

The old man raised his head. Sunlight broke through the clouds and lit his eyes. Like a halo his woolly white hair framed a sweet brown face.

"Don't nobody own me," the old man said. "I be a free man."

Pascal stared when he saw the white man reach down by the carriage seat, then he covered his mouth to keep from screaming.

With another curse the young man shot Mr. Freedman. A puff of dust skipped from the road, and the old man jerked and fell back across the gurgling ditch. He slid down against the bushes and was as still as death.

Pascal stared at the white man, who blew his smoking pistol before putting it back and then started his carriage and drove on. Was that how it was when the overseer shot Mama? Did white people have no feelings? How could that man just kill somebody and drive on? Pascal wished he could put his stick in those fancy rolling carriage wheels and break every spoke!

The sound of the pistol had silenced woodland birds and insects. Only the water in the ditch gurgled its melody, now a sorrowful sound.

Trembling, Pascal turned and wiped his eyes. Sure, they were free. But if nobody allowed their freedom, what would owning land mean? This kind of freedom was as bad as slavery.

With a sniff, Gideon said, "Looks like here be somebody else I gotta bury." Gideon had tears in his eyes, too.

First he smoothed the man's coat, then set the man's battered straw hat on his chest. Pascal leaned on his stick. Nelly climbed down. Twisting her braids, she crept over to stare. "Where's he bleeding?" she asked.

After she spoke, Mr. Freedman opened his eyes. Leaning on an elbow, he scrambled to get up. Nelly gasped, and Pascal almost fell as he stepped back.

"I suppose that pistol shot gave you a scare," said Mr. Freedman. "I learned to jerk away and play dead. But sometimes the bullet bites." He showed an old leg wound at his ankle.

Pascal noticed that besides the battered straw hat, the old man was well dressed. Of course he needed the battered hat. Colored folks couldn't dress too decent or white folks would punish them for acting uppity.

Gideon held out his hand. "How to do, Mister Freedman. Would you join us for supper? We ain't got much 'cause we're traveling."

Pascal thought, My brother may be mean sometimes, but he ain't stingy. Gideon would break one crumb into two to share.

"Thank ye." Mr. Freedman pointed. "I have a bag of carpenter tools I left hid down the road. I been trying to catch up to you young people. I be right back." He seemed limber for an old man. When he returned, they set up camp in the woods. Mr. Freedman and Gideon talked about the forty acres.

"Nelly, Pascal," said Gideon as he set stones in a circle for a fireplace, "I think we'll take some time out and rest here. Georgia be less than a day away."

In a low voice Nelly told Pascal, "Now your brother got Mister Freedman to talk to. That's why he be taking a rest."

Pascal nodded. Sure. Gideon wanted to boast about his plans for forty acres; he needed to make his dreams real with an airing. Gideon seemed bold, but he might be frightened.

Pascal remembered what Mama used to say about Gideon: *All bark and no bite.* His brother acted big, but "when push came to shove," he sometimes needed help. Well, that was Pascal's job. He'd be right at Gideon's side, he and Nelly. Together they were family.

Mr. Freedman shared their bread. He had bought salt pork at a store to go in a pot of boiled cabbage. It was good to have a hot meal, thanks to Nelly's pot. Usually they had eaten the cabbage raw. Pascal's stomach felt better than it had in two weeks.

That evening they sat in a circle around a fire as clouds playfully tugged the sun lower in the sky. Nelly asked Pascal, "Do you feel free?"

He scratched his side. "I don't know."

Mr. Freedman said, "Freedom is all about having dignity. I don't have to feel shame. If I don't accept a curse, it returns to the curser. Since nobody owns me, I can come and go. And do good for folks as I see fit."

"I think freedom be all about owning land and having people look at you with respect," said Gideon, leaning against a tree.

"Then you ain't free yet," Nelly said.

Gideon scowled at her.

"What you think freedom be, Nelly?" Pascal asked, thinking that talking like this must be part of it.

"It be here," Nelly said, touching her chest. "Freedom's something inside you. I feel free like a bird."

"You look like a girl," said Pascal with a smile.

"That's all hooey," said Gideon. He hit the dirt with a stone. "You ain't nobody till you own land."

Pascal lay back and put his hands behind his head. "Maybe freedom's different things for different people. I think it be something small that grow like a seed planted. Every day I feel a little more free." He groaned. "But there be so much I don't know. Them white people tried to keep us dumb and helpless."

"You and Nelly can go to schools now," said Mr. Freedman quickly. "They setting up schools for the coloreds and poor whites of the South."

"Yes, sir, I'd like that." Pascal thought learning must be part of being free, because slaves weren't allowed to learn before — though secretly he had learned to read.

"They got women from the North — volunteers white and colored — being sent to teach former slaves," Mr. Freedman said. " 'Tis a time of glory, children."

Pascal looked down at his leg. "I'd be a heap more free without this lame leg." He stared at the ground. Nelly could move so smoothly, so gracefully, and he couldn't. What could owning land do for a crippled colored boy? With a puzzled look Nelly sat staring at him. She began twisting her braids.

"You folks know any abolitionists?" Mr. Freedman asked.

"No, sir," said Gideon.

"I talked at their meetings. They be people what worked to stop slavery. Now they gonna help us freedmens."

Where they sat, the gurgle of the ditch was background music for mosquito whines and cricket chirps. Occasionally a woodland sparrow exploded into song. Sunbeams danced on their faces, and a scent of broken pine branch spiced the air. Pascal heard people passing on the road above, but their campsite was hidden.

"On our farm," began Gideon, "the sun ain't gonna rise till we be ready to open our eyes. And we won't even have to pick up our hoes to chop cotton."

"We won't?" asked Nelly.

"No, ma'am. Every morning that hoe gonna stand 'at attention' all by itself."

"Will we have an overseer?" Pascal asked.

"Only overseer gonna be the sun by day and the moon by night," Gideon said. "And," he added quickly, "we ain't working late no more. Gonna nap at the heat of day, and dance in the dark of night. On my farm."

Mr. Freedman looked confused.

"And tell about the boll weevils," said Nelly, giggling.

"Should a boll weevil dare come near our cotton," Gideon said, "I'll whip him at a tree for shame."

Mr. Freedman began to smile.

"You think we gonna have trouble finding

our farm?" Nelly asked. "After all, in the Bible the Hebrew children wandered in the desert for forty years."

"And you know why?" asked Gideon.

"Why?" asked Pascal.

"'Cause they kept on grumbling. We doing it right. Ain't no complaining on this march to the promised land. And you know why the sun be shining?"

Nelly shook her head. "Why, Gideon?"

"It be laughing at the white masters, and cheering for the colored freedmens. That be why. The whole heavens am in jubilee." He glanced up. "Can't you tell?"

Pascal threw back his head. The clouds in the darkening sky were like white chicken feathers floating free. He caught his breath and held it. Yes, the heavens were in jubilee!

But he heard a commotion, people talking.

Mr. Freedman climbed the hillside to look down the road. Waving, he ran back. Pascal heard some voices call, "Look! There's someone else to tell about freedom. Come on, colored people, we'll hold a camp here!"

Pascal felt a fist grab in his gut. What now?

Chapter Four

Three white men slid down the hill. About twenty-five colored men and women followed, making a trod-down path to the campsite. Pascal recognized some of the people from the road.

He stared at all the young men. One of them could be his brother. None looked like Mama, but then a brother could possibly look like Papa, too. Their Papa had lived and died on another plantation. Pascal had hardly ever seen him.

The first white man down the hill was heavyset, wore a fancy black waistcoat, and carried a top hat. The other gentlemen were in new-looking brown suits with derbys. Who were these people? Pascal wondered.

"Ladies and gentlemen," called the first man in a rapid Northern accent, "I am Mr. McPherson. Good news! This is the first meeting of the Union League club, and you are all members."

Pascal had trouble following his words. Nelly's mouth hung open. The man smiled and waved at all of them. Why was the white man being so friendly? Mr. McPherson shouted, "The War Between the States is over!" The three white men clapped.

Silently, the colored people stood staring at them. Pascal wondered: What if these men were sent to catch them? No one was going to take him or Nelly or Gideon back! He gripped his walking stick. No one would trick him out of his freedom.

"Union armies fought for your freedom," called Mr. McPherson, pointing to them. "President Lincoln wrote the Emancipation Proclamation that freed you." He paused, pointing a finger at the people. "Now, who freed you?"

Without hesitation everyone said, "God!" Everyone knew God had answered their prayers, thought Pascal.

The white man blinked, his face flushed red, and he tried again. "Who wrote the Emancipation Proclamation?"

"President Lincoln, sir," Pascal said loudly. He had heard the master cussing about that Proclamation, but he hadn't known that it meant freedom.

"Father Abraham, sir."

"Mr. Lincoln, sir," Nelly called, bumping Pascal's elbow.

"Then," asked Mr. McPherson, "who freed you?"

"God!" they all said louder.

"Yes, yes," Mr. McPherson said, wiping his face with a large white handkerchief. "President Lincoln's party is the Republican Party. Who wants to be a Republican?"

No one spoke. The white man looked around. "You don't want to be Democrats, do you? Which party do you want?"

A party? No one spoke. Pascal wondered if these were like white people's birthday parties. Would there be cake?

"The Democratic Party is the party of the white masters. The Republican Party is the party of Abraham Lincoln. The party that freed you." Mr. McPherson wiped his face again.

One of the other white men said in a soft Southern accent, "I was a slave owner, but I freed my slaves and joined the Republican Party. People 'round here call me scalawag, but I needed bread for my children. Y'all understand that?"

Pascal leaned against a tree trunk to listen. This meeting was unbelievable. These white men were *asking* colored people,

41

rather than *ordering* them. Was that what freedom was about?

Mr. McPherson said, "The Republican Party will give you orphanages, hospitals, asylums, schools . . ."

At the word *school,* Pascal clapped, and a second later Nelly joined him. Ain't we uppity, he thought, but he felt good clapping. Some people shifted and stared at them. Others began to murmur, to move around, to loosen up.

"Look around, ladies and gentlemen," called Mr. McPherson. "Abandoned farms, war ruins, open homestead land. Well, the Republican Party wants to give forty acres and maybe a mule to every former slave family." He waved a newspaper. "You don't have to run away to the North anymore."

Gideon raised his arms and shouted, "Forty acres and maybe a mule, now that be freedom!" Several people joined him clapping. Pascal liked Republicans now. Where did they hold the parties?

Mr. McPherson pointed to a man with a book. "You men step over there to register Republican."

The evening sky had darkened into purple shades. Crickets chirped, and the three-quarter moon wore a smug, glowing smile.

As men were registering, Mr. McPherson read aloud from his newspaper. When Gideon returned, Pascal whispered, "Did you hear him? They want us slaves to have land, and they want to punish the white masters. It's called *Reconstruction.*"

"Then it must be the living truth," Gideon said softly. Pascal frowned at his brother. So Gideon hadn't been so sure after all.

When every man had been registered, Mr. McPherson told them: "People say we Northerners are carpetbaggers coming down here to make money off the Southland. But the Republican Party is paying me to organize in the South. It's a job." He smiled.

"Now you are all registered Republicans," he said. "What are you?"

"Free," shouted the people. "Free!"

Mr. McPherson wiped his face again. "Remember," he called as he picked up a carpetbag to leave, "tell all your friends and family to register Republican."

Pascal wondered if being Republican got you better land. He was glad Gideon had registered. Forty acres and maybe a mule seemed like a sure thing now that General Sherman, President Lincoln, Republicans, and Union League people all wanted them to have it. He could almost taste that land of milk and honey!

The white men were leaving. It looked as if there was no food at this party. Pascal sure wished there was cake. One white man started up the hill. At the top Pascal saw him put his hand behind his ear. "Night riders," he called. "Run!"

Chapter Five

The Republican organizers and the crowd of freed slaves scattered. Nelly scrambled high in a tree; Pascal dived into the bushes. He watched Gideon and Mr. Freedman tossing tree branches and kicking firewood and stones. When they finished and hurried off, the place no longer looked like a campsite.

Pascal got a bold idea. Head high, he made snarling screeching sounds like wildcats fighting. When he stopped snarling, the woodlands were quiet.

From up on the road he heard a creaking wagon sound and the sound of galloping horses overtaking the wagon. The cantering riders halted.

Pascal saw that a small farm wagon carried four yellow-haired children leaning over the side. A man and a woman sat in front. The woman held an infant. Mattresses were piled across ladder-back chairs to form a sleeping room in back. It seemed to be a family of war refugees.

The men on horses carried whips, and shotguns rested across their saddles. A fist balled up in Pascal's stomach, and he began to tremble.

"Have y'all seen about thirty Negroes on the road?" one rider asked. Pascal stared at his bushy eyebrows.

"No, sir," said the man driving the wagon. "We're looking for the road to Georgia."

"Y'all seen any Yankee white men?" the other rider asked. "We hear Northerners are stirring up trouble among the darkies. Making promises to them."

"No, sir, but we'd be much obliged if you could tell us the direction of the nearest bridge?" The wagon driver had a low, mountain-man accent. The children stared at the riders.

"You see any darkies," said the second man, "y'all tell them to go back to their masters. Y'all tell them go back for spring planting." He turned to the other rider. "Those were wildcats we heard."

Pascal nodded. For years he had listened to and practiced animal calls, and it hadn't been in vain. He had thought it would come in handy one day. Now his animal sounds had saved them.

However, the white men sounded desperate. The slaves were seeking new lives, and the masters needed workers. Would the masters offer to pay their former slaves?

Patting her infant, the woman leaned forward. "Now that the slaves are freed," she asked, "what do they get paid?" The lady had asked the question for Pascal.

One rider raised his fist, but the other man put his hand over it. "Ma'am," he said, removing his hat, "we ain't about to pay Negroes to work when we own them in the first place, and we can whip them into working without wages in the second place."

"We're shooting the uppity ones and bringing back the submissive ones," said the other rider. "Good evening, y'all."

As they rode off, one rider turned in the saddle and called, "Remember, tell any darkies you see that the night riders will get them if they don't go back."

The riders galloped off, lit by moonlight as they rode.

"Pa, you can roll the wagon down over there," the oldest girl said. She pointed ahead to a broad path.

Her father flicked the reins, rode to the path, and sat staring downhill. "I suppose that's where the Negroes were," he told his wife in a low voice.

The oldest girl jumped off the wagon and walked along the ditch. When she came to Pascal, she wrapped her long blue skirt around her legs and squatted.

"Evening, sir," she said. "My name's Judith. What's your name?" The other three children crawled over the side of the wagon and stood staring after their sister.

"I be Pascal, miss."

"Well, Pascal, we're Bibbs. Come meet my ma and pa."

Taking his hand, Judith dragged him to her parents. "I found this boy in the bushes, Pa."

"Would you mind if we pulled our wagon down there?" asked Mr. Bibb, pointing downhill.

Pascal shook his head. "No, sir," he said.

"We're from Tennessee," Judith said. "I'm twelve years old, and these here are my brothers. Matthew, he's six years old. Say howdy, Matthew. He's shy. Don't talk much never. And this here is Mark."

She frowned. "Ma, how old you reckon Mark is?"

Mrs. Bibb was all smiles as her husband helped her down from the wagon seat. "Bless you, son. I'm so very very very happy to meet you. If Matthew is six, I reckon Mark is four. My, how the years fly."

Pascal reached for her outstretched hand and shook it. "My name be Pascal, ma'am."

"Well. Pascal. Ain't that a nice name, Pa?"

Mr. Bibb frowned. "You reckon it's a Bible name?"

"It means something to do with Easter, sir," said Pascal.

"Well, that is fine," said Mr. Bibb, smiling now. "It don't hurt to have the Lord's blessing in a Bible name."

"And," Judith said, "this here is little Naomi. She used to be the baby, but now Daniel is the baby. How old you reckon Naomi is, Ma?"

"Naomi? Well, she was born about a year and a half after Mark. You're a smart girl, Judith, you figure it."

While Mrs. Bibb picked up wood, Naomi held her mother's skirt and sucked her thumb. Mr. Bibb bustled about feeding the horses from feed bags and unhitching the wagon.

Pascal was amazed at these white people who treated him like a person, not like a slave. Maybe the world was changing after all. But where were Gideon and Mr. Freedman?

After Mr. Bibb fed the two brown horses, he pulled the wagon across the ditch and downhill. The boys and Naomi rode inside.

Judith ran around helping her mother prepare a fire.

Mrs. Bibb pointed to the wagon. "These here are our belongings for a new life, Pascal. A cannonball destroyed our old rented farmhouse. We have seeds for spring planting, too. Mr. Bibb and me are fixing to get forty acres for a farm of our own." She balanced a coffeepot and pans on the firestones and began mixing ground corn.

Forty acres for them, too? Pascal frowned.

Nelly climbed down from the tree. Pascal introduced her, and she began stirring corn for Mrs. Bibb.

Soon the campfire leaped in yellow flames. The little girl sucked her thumb and rested her head against her mother's skirt. Like shadows, the boys clung to their father.

Judith, however, tapped Pascal and beckoned to Nelly, "Bet you can't find me." She ran off giggling. Pascal didn't feel like playing. He had started to worry about Gideon and Mr. Freedman. Where were they? And what if these white people took the last land?

Judith called from the woods. "Can't find me." Nelly giggled and ran. Pascal called, "I see you, Miss Judith." Her blue flour-sack dress shone in the moonlight.

The cool, damp night made Pascal shiver.

Big bullfrogs croaked, and tiny tree frogs piped shrilly. Pascal slapped at mosquitoes and tried not to scratch their bites.

He pointed to the road and asked, "How come you saw me up there, Miss Judith?"

"Don't call me Miss Judith, just Judith. I'm mighty good at finding people hidden," she said. "We had a limestone cave on the hill farm Pa rented back in Tennessee. Wasn't our land rightly, but the Lord said, 'Free the captives.' So almost every week we hid slaves who were running away, and I was the one who found them and took them to our cave."

"Oh," said Pascal, "are you abolitionists?"

"No," she said, "we're Baptists."

The cheerful fire crackled, and Pascal enjoyed the smell of fresh pinewood burning. Mrs. Bibb called them to supper.

The Bibbs shared yellow corn mush with salted pork fat in chips. It was thick and hot. After cabbage and bread for two weeks, this meal was sumptuous. Pascal sucked at the chips of meat as long as he could before swallowing. He rubbed each mouthful of corn with his tongue to enjoy the juicy taste.

After supper Mr. Bibb opened the Bible and read by firelight. From a psalm he read: "'. . . do good, seek peace and follow after it.'" That was like what Mama always talked about — peace and joy, Pascal thought, but he hadn't been able to save Mama from being killed. Clutching his stick and frowning, he lay near the fire to sleep.

"No, no, no," called Mrs. Bibb. "Joseph, get down a mattress right away for the boy and his sister."

The mattress was soft and smelled sweet like the dry grass inside. This family's kindness astonished Pascal.

When all was quiet, he stretched out, and a pebble struck his shoulder. He glanced up to see Judith peeking between slats of the wagon. She wiggled her fingers. He wiggled his fingers back and closed his eyes to listen to night sounds so he could imitate them. The milky fog seemed to make the night calls louder.

Nelly touched him. "You see what they be like?" she asked in a whisper.

Raising his head, he peeked at the wagon. The Bibb family seemed to be asleep. "Like what?" he asked.

"Well, Judith dances on her toes."

"So?"

"That's about freedom, Pascal. White people be used to freedom. We can learn from them."

"Oh." He shrugged. The point wasn't quite clear to him.

"Free people ain't used to worrying about a master. They can be . . . any way they want to be. Free!"

Pascal frowned. With night riders trying to catch them, they weren't free yet. He pulled his walking stick closer. He and Gideon might have to fight for their forty acres, but he didn't want to discourage Nelly. Soon she began to breathe slowly, and he fell asleep also.

The next morning Pascal helped the Bibbs shove their wagon uphill. They put the horses in the harness to pull the wagon across the ditch. In the east a lavender-streaked dawn slowly emerged. Pascal pointed and said, "Look at that, y'all."

There was a rose-colored explosion among the clouds as the sun broke over the tree line. A dancing, smiling Judith raised her arms. "Praise the Lord!" she called. Nelly stared at her.

"Come with us," called Mr. Bibb. "We aiming for the bridge over the Savannah and into Georgia." Judith beckoned for Pascal and Nelly to climb on the wagon with them.

Pascal explained: "My brother should be back for us right soon." Where were Gideon and Mr. Freedman, anyway?

Chapter Six

Pascal and Nelly drew a circle in the dirt and took turns hitting two marbles out of the circle with the third marble. But Pascal kept glancing around. He was troubled, uneasy about Gideon, though he didn't want to worry Nelly. When Gideon and Mr. Freedman finally climbed up the hill, Pascal leaped up in relief.

"Come on down," Gideon called. "There be a lower road that lead right to the Savannah."

The children took their bags and slid through scratchy brambles. Pascal felt pleased to be on the way again. The lower road was little more than two wagon ruts, but Gideon pointed to a line of trees in the distance.

"Georgia's right over there."

Mr. Freedman said, "Since I be returning to Georgia myself, I might as well stay with you young people. I left to find my wife in Carolina." He sighed. "Now that I know she be dead, I'll take up my carpenter work in some Georgia town."

Pascal and Nelly walked in single file. This rutted road took watching to keep from tripping. As they walked, Nelly said, "You used your stick to trip Master and break things, but sometimes I be mean to get back at Master, too."

Pascal raised his eyebrows. "You? How?"

"You know them cockleburs?"

He nodded.

"Everytime I made Master's bed, I put a handful in there. The missus scold him for bringing them in from the field." She giggled.

"His desk chair, too?" asked Pascal.

Her mouth dropped open. "How'd you know?"

"I seen him jump up cussing. Didn't know you put them there." They giggled.

Pascal rubbed his weak hand and said, "Every morning I brought Master his coffee, hot and black, the way he like it."

She nodded.

"But before I took it in to him, I spit in it." He snickered softly. "Lordy, but Master be mean: starving folks, beating folks, working folks till they drop. White folks should be glad we free so they don't got to be so mean no more." Nodding, Nelly skipped a step.

"I tripped so often carrying that basket of eggs from the henhouse, the overseer threatened to sell me," she said. "Broke every egg. Then Master made me work in the Big House. He say he want a pretty little girl around him." She groaned. "I be so happy to leave Master before I growed any bigger!" Pascal took her hand and squeezed it. Terrible things happened to pretty slave girls; he was glad Nelly had escaped.

After a while he asked, "You know why chickens lay eggs?"

"No, why?"

"'Cause if they dropped them, they'd break."

"Get on, Pascal," Nelly said, giggling. "What you want to do when you grow up?"

"Farm with Gideon, I reckon." Pascal sighed. "With some more schooling, I could be a bookkeeper for the family farm. I know reading and writing some. Master spent a heap of time on the books for his plantation."

Nelly nodded. "I could be a store clerk or a seamstress. But I hate sewing 'cause my fingers always bleed. So, I'll be a store clerk."

They ran to catch up with Gideon and Mr. Freedman.

"I love the smell of wood," said Mr. Freedman. "Been lucky to do carpenter work all my life. Master hired me out, and I learned my craft from a good African man." He pointed. "That's a rickety bridge, Gideon. There's a better bridge downriver. Plenty bridges cross the Savannah River."

They broke through trees, and Pascal stared at the sparkling water. Sunshine danced on tiny blue ripples. On the river-bank fishermen had left smelly fish heads that were covered with buzzing green-bottle flies. Gideon headed for the nearby bridge, but Pascal saw holes along it.

"I be crossing here," said Gideon. "I ain't waiting another second to pass over to Georgia and order my land and mule."

Mr. Freedman took Nelly's hand. "Unless you planning to swim, you ought to come with us to the next bridge, Gideon."

Nelly and Mr. Freedman walked on down the road. With one hand she was twisting her braid and frowning. Pascal started to walk with them but stopped. He had to stick by Gideon. Keep him out of trouble.

"Come on," said Gideon. "Let them lazy good-for-nothings go to an easy bridge." Pascal winced. How could his brother say things like that about Nelly and Mr. Freedman?

He watched as Gideon picked his way over rotten boards. Halfway across the river, a board dropped and he fell. He was swinging by a long plank like a child hanging from a weeping willow branch.

Pascal yelled for help, but the others were far gone by then so he limped out onto the bridge himself. Beneath him he saw the river through holes in the rotten bridge. The water was rapid and deep.

Soon, because of broken boards, he had to creep forward on hands and knees. Pushing his stick ahead with his weak arm, he prayed as he tested boards. Finally, he reached the place where Gideon hung from the plank.

"Get rope," said Gideon. Sweat poured down his face.

Pascal looked around. "What rope? Climb up the board, one hand over the other." Pascal hooked the base of the rotten board with his walking stick.

Hand over hand, Gideon pulled himself up. Swinging by one hand, he caught at another plank, but it ripped loose. The board splashed in the river to shimmy on the surface and sink slowly. As a safer measure, Gideon reached for Pascal, who lay flat on his stomach. Pascal grasped his brother's hand and backed up. He was so frightened he could hardly think. Slowly Gideon pulled himself up. Panting and sweating, he lay on his stomach until Pascal helped him rise to his hands and knees.

Slowly Gideon followed Pascal, crawling back along the bridge. Placing his stick across the boards, Pascal slid it ahead of himself, testing the way. Soon Gideon stood, but Pascal kept crawling. Wiping his face, Gideon strode ahead and waited on the road for Pascal.

When he reached the rutted road, Pascal said nothing, but he felt hot in the face. He might have lost his brother, who was his only family, and the hope of their farm, too. With no family, no farm, and nothing else, he and Nelly'd be lost!

"That was a good bridge, except for that one spot," said Gideon. "We would of been across before Nelly and Mister Freedman, I bet. That was a good enough bridge." Gideon walked on.

Pascal slid his clothes sack on his stick and followed. Now he knew why Mama worried about Gideon. *Too bold for his britches,* she used to say.

When he glanced up, his brother had walked far ahead. Soon Pascal heard voices around a bend in the rutted road. With caution he hid in nearby high grass and crawled on his hands and knees.

He heard Gideon saying, "You ain't scaring me. I been a soldier and I traveled and I know all about our freedom. Nobody owns me now and nobody will."

He saw that a better road connected with the narrow, rutted one they had followed. A white man sat astride his horse, listening to Gideon. The man's shoulders were hunched, his hands fisted.

Pascal groaned to himself. Was his brother trying to play Mr. Freedman's trick? Since the white man's back was to him, Pascal slipped behind boulders along the roadside. The horse grew nervous, pawed, and glanced back, but the rider was intent on cussing Gideon.

"You will come back with me or die!" shouted the white man, shaking his fist. "Now walk."

"I ain't doing what no white man tells me, never no more," said Gideon. "I be studying to get me forty acres and a mule." He took a deep breath and added, "And I be a Republican like President Abraham Lincoln."

"Lincoln's dead, and you'll be dead, too," said the man. Pascal was almost up to him now. Bareheaded, the man wore tan riding breeches torn at the knee, and a patched topcoat.

Rising up, Pascal raised his stick and whacked the horse across its flank. It reared. After a second blow, the horse galloped up the connecting road, its rider yelling and clinging to his saddle.

With that, Pascal passed Gideon and limped as fast as he could along the narrow road. He felt scared and angry, too. How foolish could Gideon be? Suppose that white man had carried a gun? He heard Gideon catch up and stride along.

"I told him, didn't I?" Gideon asked, grinning.

Pascal groaned. "Walls of Jericho! No wonder Mama used to worry about you."

"But, didn't I tell him off?"

Pascal shouted, "Gideon! I saved you from that man!"

"You save me?" said Gideon. "I didn't need no saving. You just a crooked-leg child." He laughed. "I told that white man off. I ain't crawling for no white man no more never!" He stooped and carried Pascal piggyback.

Pascal clasped his brother's neck. That day he had saved Gideon, not once, but twice, and his brother had only made fun of him.

But Pascal felt pleased. He had always known he was brave, and he had proved it to himself again. Fighting Goliath, David in the Bible had a slingshot; fighting slavery, Pascal had his walking stick. He'd keep Gideon safe. It was good to be needed.

Gideon's long-legged stride covered ground rapidly. Soon Pascal saw Nelly and Mr. Freedman. "Gideon," Pascal said, "that man said President Lincoln be dead. You reckon he's right?"

Chapter Seven

Shadows of afternoon cooled the April day. From piggyback on Gideon's shoulders, Pascal could see that Mr. Freedman and Nelly were waiting for them.

A covered bridge like a long barn loomed ahead. The wood was patched, and red paint peeled from the sides. However, when a carriage creaked out of the bridge, Pascal knew it must be safe. He slid from Gideon's shoulders.

A horse and rider followed the carriage, and the rider waved a newspaper at them. "The president's been shot, boys," he called. "Bad news for you Negroes."

A woman dressed in Sunday clothes leaned out the carriage window. "What did you say, sir?"

"President Lincoln's been shot!"

Clutching his stick, Pascal walked close to the carriage and listened to the rider tell the lady the news. Gideon, Nelly, and Mr. Freedman stood by the entrance to the covered bridge.

"Yes, ma'am," the man said. "President Abraham Lincoln was shot in the back of his head at Ford's Theatre in Washington. They don't expect him to live." He shook the newspaper. "Hot off the wires, and only two days old."

"When, sir?" she asked.

"Shot April fourteenth. Good Friday, ma'am."

"Well," she said, pulling her head back into the carriage, "it serves him right. He couldn't just go around freeing people's property."

The man tipped his derby to her and folded his paper. Pascal ran over to tell the others. His voice trembled, and he swallowed hard. He wanted to ask, *What about our forty acres?* but he didn't want to worry Nelly.

"What happens now?" Gideon asked.

The man overheard him. "Vice President Andrew Johnson takes over as president, boys," he said as he rode away.

"President Lincoln ain't gonna die," Gideon said, stomping his boot. "I knew a soldier shot in the neck who lived."

Mr. Freedman said softly, "The man said

shot in the back of his head. That be a heap more serious."

Pascal took a deep breath and exhaled slowly. President Lincoln wanted to give them land. If President Lincoln died, what would happen to their family farm? Their future?

Nelly stared at them sadly. "We should pray for our president," she said. "Ease his way into glory, if that be the Lord's will."

The men removed their hats, and they all stood in a circle with heads bowed. Pascal closed his eyes and prayed, not so much for the wounded president, but for them. A late afternoon breeze whistled sadly like a funeral flute. Tree leaves rustled.

As they entered the dark, covered bridge, Gideon asked the question Pascal had been thinking: "You reckon if President Lincoln dies, they'll still give me my forty acres?"

Pascal felt that squeezing fist in his guts. Maybe getting that family farm was impossible now. They'd soon find out. Poor Gideon. Poor Pascal and Nelly. He decided to make his brother feel good.

"Sure," he said loudly. "President Lincoln's vice president must be a Republican, too. Seems like the Republicans, the Union League people, and General Sherman are all for giving us forty acres and maybe a mule."

With a sigh, Gideon strode ahead of them.

The covered bridge had occasional windows on each side but in spite of the windows, the inside was dark and gloomy. Pascal didn't like to be closed up. He felt as if he could hardly catch his breath. He held Nelly's hand until they walked out.

They were in Georgia now. Sunshine at the end of the covered bridge was welcome. After he limped out, blinking, he glanced around quickly and thought of something: Good Friday, Saturday, Sunday.

"Walls of Jericho!" he said, "y'all know what today be?"

Mr. Freedman raised an eyebrow.

"Easter Sunday! Today be Easter Sunday, and we be in River Stop, Georgia," said Pascal, pointing to a sign.

"Well, glory be," said Mr. Freedman, "I heard my daughter had a child what was sold to work in River Stop. Guess I be going to look for her in the morning."

"Y'all," Gideon said, "I be scouting for a campsite."

"Come back soon," Pascal called. It seemed as if Gideon was always leaving them. He turned to Nelly. "Know why Saturday and Sunday be strong days?"

"Strong?" she asked.

"'Cause Monday through Friday be weak days."

Nelly snickered and whispered the town's name.

"You know anybody from River Stop?" Pascal asked her.

"River Stop been calling my name all my born days." Her honey-brown eyes sparkled. "All these freedom-ringing places, they been calling me." Twirling her skirt, she smiled.

Pascal frowned. "How you know they been calling you?"

"It be a special mystery thing."

"You saying you always knew you'd be here?"

"I'm here, ain't I?"

Mr. Freedman strolled over to talk to some men sitting by the bridge. Pascal stretched out on his back in the warm, sunny grass. What a day this had been: They were in Georgia now, and soon they might have that land.

He felt something crawling on his cheek; something crawling on his arm. Her back turned, Nelly sat chewing a blade of grass.

Pascal was suspicious. Lying on his side, he stretched an arm out and squinted his eyes. He saw the blade of grass dance on his arm. Grunting, he pretended to be asleep.

When he thought she was off guard, he jumped up and yelled, "Gotcha!" Nelly jerked her arm back and laughed.

"You looked like you be asleep."

"You tickled me!" He started to chase her, and she ran circles around him. Finally he sat and rubbed his lame leg. What kind of freedom was having a lame leg and letting a girl outrun you? How he wished for two good legs and arms!

As they sat, he told Nelly about Gideon falling through the bridge, and Gideon talking back to the man on horseback.

"You be brave," she said, hugging her knees. Pascal sat straighter in the glow of Nelly's admiration. Gideon had called him a "crooked-leg." It made him feel like a nobody, but if they could have a family farm, he would be somebody. Gideon said so.

As if she knew what he was thinking, Nelly said, "I be worried about your brother. If they don't give him this here land, what's gonna happen to him?"

What's gonna happen to you and me? Pascal wondered.

As evening shadows crept along the riverbank, Gideon returned. He led them to a rocky ledge on a piney woods hillside. Under the ledge an opening led into a shallow limestone cave. Pascal had always dreamed of hiding in a cave, and this cave was perfect. Fragrant-scented pine trees above and below them on the hillside were covered with long-needle puffs of green. The bare ground was ankle-deep in brown pine needles. No one could tell they were in the cave.

That night Pascal slept well, sheltered from the wind and dew. Awaking early, he squatted in the cave entrance where he could look over the pine forest clear down to the Savannah River. Open spaces always made him feel good.

After a breakfast of water and one small chunk of bread each, Gideon announced he would go into town to ask about a Freedmen's Bureau.

Mr. Freedman put on his straw hat. "I be looking around town myself. Some gentlemen told me where my granddaughter just might be."

Nelly winked at Pascal. After the grown-ups were gone, she asked, "Can you fish?"

"If I can dig some worms."

"We gonna have a real supper when they come back." She pulled the pot out of her sack.

Pascal knelt on rocks where sunlight playfully kissed his face from time to time. He had dug worms, and fish swam up to snap at them. He used his potato sack to net the fish. In two hours of patient waiting and fast snatching, he caught five nice-size silvery fish.

"There," he said. "I thought I could do that." He felt like a man, handing over fish for Nelly to cook.

Nelly cleaned the fish and seasoned them with chopped wild onion. "I be keeping them cool in my pot," she said, setting the pot in cold water between rocks.

That afternoon Pascal saw Mr. Freedman come back with a tall girl who was carrying a bundle. "Pascal and Nelly," said Mr. Freedman, "this here be my granddaughter Gladness, who wants to join us. She remembered me from when she been a child. I just called her name, and she packed up and left for freedom."

Gladness held out her hand. "How do you?"

Pascal nodded and shook hands. He hadn't expected her to be pretty as a daisy flower. Gladness's smile — white teeth in a dark brown face — was like a bright sun streak from dark skies.

Gladness helped Nelly boil the fish, and they feasted.

As they ate, Gladness rubbed her arms,

took deep breaths, and glanced toward the sky, smiling as if she could hardly believe she was free. She seemed thankful to be with them. It made Pascal remember how he had felt when Gideon had come for him and Nelly. In spite of the troubles they were having finding their farm, these were glory days, exciting jubilee times. If only Mama had lived.

That evening Gideon didn't come back. All night Pascal worried about him. Had his brother gotten himself in trouble again? Should he have gone with Gideon?

Chapter Eight

The next morning Pascal felt the ground shaking as Gideon came leaping downhill in bounding jumps, crashing against pine branches. Nearly to the cave, he took off his blue army cap and threw it in the air with a loud "whoop!"

"I found it, I found it!" he called, bending at the waist to catch his breath. Gideon pointed behind him.

"In the town over yonder there's an office read: 'Bureau of Refugees, Freedmen, and Abandoned Lands.' Then it read: 'General Oliver O. Howard, Commissioner'!" He waved his arms and shouted, "The Freedmen's Bureau! Where they be giving out forty acres and maybe a mule!"

Raising his eyebrows, Mr. Freedman nodded to Gladness. Softly he said, "There be a heap of angry white men against the coloreds. Ain't gonna be easy for you. You really studying to ask for them forty acres?"

Closing his eyes, Pascal knew what Mr. Freedman meant. Only someone as bold as Gideon would think he could get forty acres for a family farm. Being landowners after being slaves! That was almost unbelievable.

Maybe being bold like Gideon and Mama was a good thing. But then, Pascal thought, he had saved Gideon twice, and Mama was dead. It was good to be careful, too.

"Sure as God's in his heaven, I'll have me forty acres!" Gideon threw his cap on the ground.

Mr. Freedman pointed to himself, then to the cave where his bag lay. "Not only can I farm, but I got hammer, nails, and saw. I be a better than middling carpenter-builder. You be needing a house and barn, I reckon. Could you use me?"

Next Mr. Freedman pointed to Gladness. Pascal saw his brother's surprise. Gideon hadn't noticed Gladness before.

"And my granddaughter Gladness here, she's a healer from the wise old people. She know herbs for making poultices. Could she help?" Pascal thought her dimpled smile as she said hello reflected the meaning of her wonderful name.

"Sure, sure," whispered Gideon in a hoarse voice. "Forty acres is a lot of land. I never thought as to how I could farm it alone. Thank you."

Pascal watched his brother glance at Gladness again. She was tall for a girl, about Gideon's age, and pretty as a redbird in a pine tree. His brother seemed dazed by her beauty. Gideon wiped his face with his sleeve and seemed to recover.

Chopping the air with his hands, he said, "Now this the way it be: There be four families asking there already, a family of white folks with a wagon, and three colored families with children along. I need all of you to come for my family."

Pascal grinned. It was true, they were a big family now!

Gideon straightened up. "Ain't nobody saying I ain't old enough, 'cause I'm tall enough!" No one challenged him. "I'm a man with a family, and tomorrow morning me and my family gotta be the first ones there. We can't miss getting them forty acres."

Pascal felt that Mr. Freedman admired Gideon's spunk in asking for a farm. Pascal was proud of Gideon, and Mama would have been, too. If it was possible, his brother would get them those forty acres.

Gideon said, "I don't want Master's last name, so I'll have to find a new one." He slapped his hat on his head.

Nelly stared at Gideon and began twisting her braids.

"Come on, Gideon," Pascal said, "eat something." He touched Nelly's shoulder as she walked past to sit beside Gladness. "When you decide on a last name, I'll take it, too."

The two brothers sat in the cave entrance. Pine fragrance spiced the still air; the sun slipped behind clouds for a moment. Pascal handed his brother a chunk of bread and a tin cup of water. He was sorry Gideon had missed the fish-boil.

"Pascal," Gideon said, "we gonna own a farm, and I'm gonna be my own boss. I feel like I've crossed over to the land of milk and honey." He slapped his thigh and laughed. "Now all I need be a last name."

Pascal pointed. "Woods be a strong last name."

"River, too," Gideon said, pointing to the distant Savannah. "Gideon River. Pascal River. River reminds me," he said, "there be farms to be had on Georgia's Sea Islands, too. Ain't many going that far for land, but I hear it's open for folks."

River? "Gideon," asked Pascal, "didn't we have an older brother name of River?"

"River Jordan," said Gideon. "Ain't thought about him in years. I heard that

Mama carried on something terrible when Master sold him. I was just a baby. How come you remember?"

"Mama talked about him. He was her firstborn."

"He looked like our papa, I heard."

"I don't remember Papa." Pascal groaned. The masters had really broken up their family.

All afternoon they studied names — strong, different names.

"City," Pascal said. "Mama had the name of Jerusalem City."

"That be her first name. City? Gideon City? Pascal City?" Gideon shook his head. "Never heard of nobody name of City."

Shrugging, Pascal said, "So?" Gideon stared into the trees.

"Yes!" Gideon jumped up and pulled Pascal to his feet. "We be Jerusalem City's boys on our way to forty acres. Gideon City! Pascal City!" They laughed and hugged each other.

That evening they walked into town. The five of them sat in front of the storefront Freedmen's Bureau all night. Gideon wouldn't let anyone beat them to that land.

In early morning while it was still dark, Pascal heard a wagon that creaked in a familiar way. He stood and waved as the wagon pulled up. Mr. Bibb hitched his horses to a hitching post and said, "Come up and set a might, Pascal. Everybody's asleep but me. Did you hear that President Lincoln died?"

"No, sir. We heard he was shot." Fear and sadness choked Pascal. The worst had happened. Now what?

"It's a sad, heart-heavy time. Are you here for help?"

"Yes, sir. My brother Gideon — " Pascal stopped. "My brother Gideon *City* is asking for forty acres and maybe a mule."

He watched Gideon wake up and look around for him, so he waved from the wagon. He didn't want Gideon to worry.

"We heard about land on the Sea Islands in the ocean, but that's farther on," said Mr. Bibb. "If the land around here looks good, we may settle here. It's planting time already."

Pascal listened to him until baby Daniel woke Mrs. Bibb, then Pascal climbed down. Gideon, Mr. Freedman, Gladness, and Nelly were awake now.

When Pascal told them that President Lincoln had died, no one spoke for a long time. During their silence the sun rose over city stores in an April haze like a veil. He felt excited. This was the day they'd get that family farm. Or not. Today that veil would be pulled aside.

Pointing to the wagon, Gideon asked, "Who they be?"

"The Bibbs," said Pascal. "They be the people what talked to the night riders."

Gideon made a fist. "I shouldn't have ran. I should of told them night riders how I was free, like I told that other white man. They just out trying to scare folks. There be land out there with my name burned on it like a brand on a cow, and ain't nobody keeping me from it."

Nelly began twisting her braids.

"Gideon," Pascal said softly, "sometimes we got to talk nice to white folks and just accept things to stay alive."

Pascal hoped his brother would be respectful to the man at the Freedmen's Bureau. He hoped nothing would go wrong getting that family farm.

Chapter Nine

For over six hours Pascal breathed the dust raised by Main Street carriage wheels and horses. After a while Nelly's dress was more dusty-tan than yellow.

Pascal felt hungry, tired, and fearful. Finding a Freedmen's Bureau had been a struggle, but Gideon hadn't given up. Yet now that they were there, no one had come to serve them. Would white people actually give land to freed slaves?

The master and overseer always told Pascal, Gideon, Mama, and the other slaves that they were worthless. Every day white people told colored folks that they were good-for-nothing. Some slaves even called themselves shiftless, no good, worthless.

Mama didn't think so. One day she asked the missus, "If we colored folks be so worthless, why you pay money for us?" She'd been slapped for saying that, but Pascal remembered. That plantation had been run by slaves who cared about the crops, who knew what to do and did it.

Pascal felt that he was a brave person. Every day he told himself that. And who could be braver than Gideon, fighting for his forty acres? But sometimes Pascal wondered: Could slaves run a farm? They were smart, but were they smart enough? Pascal sighed and glanced at Nelly.

She said, "Gideon, tell Gladness about the boll weevils."

"Them bitty bugs what get in cotton?" Gladness asked.

"Any boll weevils creeping near Gideon City's farm," began Gideon, "gonna shake and shiver till they little bitty eyes fall out. Maybe till they little bitty legs fall off. And any bold enough to walk onto my field gonna be whipped at the tree."

"When we on our forty acres," Pascal added, "every morning we gonna rise up singing, and every night we gonna laugh till the moon rise, and the stars sing 'Glory to God.'"

"Gonna rest at the heat of day," said Mr. Freedman, "and eat biscuits for breakfast every day of the week."

"Our cotton won't need no color dye," Gideon said. "It gonna burst out pink and blue and yellow and red. And don't nobody need pick seeds. They gonna fall into our hands singing, 'Praise the Lord'!" Pascal smiled and tried to imagine a field of cotton in many colors.

His brother had changed. In the last couple of days it seemed that the anger inside Gideon had made him strong, not mean. He called Nelly by her name, not "good-for-nothing." And he hadn't called Pascal "crooked-leg" since the bridge.

"And," said Gideon, "ain't none of our hoes need to break."

All of them laughed. Pascal remembered hearing about hoes and rakes breaking on the plantation. After a slave got a bad beating, Master would be cussing because slaves in the fields reported all his tools broke. Master would be furious to have to buy more tools, but the slaves would grin behind his back. Pascal glanced around.

River Stop was a big town with six streets running north and south, and ten streets running east and west. People had stores and shops along Main Street.

Tapping his shoulder, Nelly made Pascal turn so she could stuff a little piece of bread in his mouth. After meals she hid food in her skirt.

"Umm," he said softly. "Where you keep

food?" He pulled out his pockets, which had no bottoms at all.

"I can sew your pockets," Nelly said, and she whipped out thread. "Where you keep your pretty pebbles?"

"My what?"

She reached in her hem pocket. "See?" She had six pebbles: one round, one long, one reddish, one tan, and two black. "Pascal," she said, "every day you got to pick a pretty pebble to appreciate the glory of the earth."

"Only six?"

"That's the fun part. When you see one even prettier, you pick it, and drop another. For the glory of the earth."

He watched her sew and turned for her to sew up his back pockets. When they were finished, a storekeeper walked out and handed them each a piece of crystal-clear rock candy. After saying, "Thank you," Nelly and Pascal sat on the wooden curb sucking.

"Seems like Christmas," said Pascal with a grin.

Nelly took her candy out and looked at it. "Bigger than Christmas," she said.

That was true, thought Pascal. For Christmas Master gave candy to each slave child, but the piece was smaller than this. "I want mine to last," he said.

For a while she was quiet. "I can't stop sucking it."

He nodded. The sugar brimmed his mouth with sweetness.

The sun was at noon when men trotted out from the hotel across the street. They went into the Bureau office and dragged tables and chairs onto the wooden sidewalk. Pascal had noticed the men peering from behind hotel curtains. Why had they been hiding?

Gideon was first in line, and Pascal stood at his elbow. Nothing would keep them from those forty acres. Nelly stood by Gladness. The barrel-shaped Bureau man finally looked at Gideon. "Can I help y'all?" asked the man.

Gideon answered, "Yes, sir." The man stared at him, then glanced up and down the street. The pencil in his hand trembled. Why were these men so nervous? Pascal wondered.

"Do you want seed?"

"Yes, sir."

"Do you want a hoe?"

"Yes, sir."

"Give him seed and a hoe," the man told his assistant. He called, "Next."

Pascal looked at Gideon. His brother's jaw hung slack, and he was shaking like a mouse in a cat's claw. After all this time, Gideon wasn't asking? Pascal had to speak up for his brother, and quick. "He want forty acres and a mule, sir."

Gideon repeated, "Forty acres and a mule, sir."

"We ain't got no mules. You want forty acres?"

"Yes, sir," Pascal said. He couldn't understand it; Gideon seemed as if a stone had bumped his head.

"Who are you?" the man asked Pascal.

"Family, sir." He pointed to Mr. Freedman, Nelly, and Gladness. "We all be his family." Walls of Jericho! he thought, we even look like family: grandfather, young couple, two children. Pascal felt a jolt of joy from tooth to toenail! "Forty acres, sir," he repeated loudly.

The man stood to stare down the street. Judith Bibb ran to Pascal and Nelly. From the corner of his eye Pascal saw Nelly take Judith's hand, and he heard them breathing behind him.

The man jerked open a box and took out a map. "Y'all know these parts?" he asked Pascal as he unfolded the map.

"Not too well, sir." Pascal squared his shoulders.

The man pointed on the map. "Along here

84

we got land don't belong to nobody. There's also land to be had on Georgia's Sea Islands. Land going for begging there." The man glanced up and said in a low voice, "Safer for you Negroes there. Where you want land?"

"South Carolina," said Gideon.

"This ain't South Carolina. This here's Georgia."

"Georgia," Gideon said. Pascal stared at him. Had his brother lost his mind?

Judith touched the map. "There's a creek and there's a lake," she said, pointing to shapes.

"We want a creek and a lake," said Pascal. He wondered how Judith knew that. She seemed so bold, so . . . free.

Gideon repeated, "Creek and lake, sir."

The man turned the map around to look. He flashed a quick smile, then checked up and down the street. "Are y'all superstitious?" he asked.

"No, sir," said Pascal. "We're Methodists."

"There's a Ghost Tree on this land."

"Yes, sir," Pascal said, "we want us a Ghost Tree."

Gideon said, "Yes, sir. Ghost Tree."

The man ran the back of his pen in a long almost rectangular shape, narrower at the top. "This here's about forty acres on Ghost Tree Lane."

"We want forty acres, sir," Gideon said.

The man glanced at numbers and wrote up a description of the land on a title. Gideon gave his name, Gideon City. Pascal City and Freedman City were added under Gideon's name. The man wrote "wife" and "girl child," but didn't include female names. Now the City family was official. Pascal hugged his weak arm.

"Now after five years y'all go register your title," the man told Gideon. "Y'all hear now?"

"Yes, sir." Pascal took the piece of paper. "Thank you, sir," he said, backing away. Carrying hoes and burlap bags of seeds, they walked down the street.

"I didn't know I'd be on the paper," Nelly said. "I be the girl child." She skipped a step.

"Walls of Jericho!" Pascal whispered, turning around. "Five miles out of this here town of River Stop we got us a family farm."

For a moment they were silent, then all at once Gideon whooped. Mr. Freedman and Gideon threw hats in the air, then ran to catch them. Nelly danced up and down. "We got forty acres!"

Pascal waved at the Bibbs and caught Gideon's arm to hurry. A lake, a creek, and a Ghost Tree?

Three blocks down the street they passed a building with a sign that read in wet blue letters: FREEDMEN'S SCHOOL.

Pascal pointed. "A school." He remembered Master bent over his farm books for hours. Here was where you could learn to be the bookkeeper for a farm.

A brown-haired white woman in a navy skirt and long-sleeved white blouse swept the wooden sidewalk. She wore an apron.

Mr. Freedman walked up to her. "Afternoon, ma'am. I reckon I'd like to know about your schoolteaching."

With pale gray eyes she looked him up and down. "I am Miss Anderson, sent here by the New England Freedmen's Union Commission," she said in a fast Northern voice.

Through the door of the storefront Pascal saw another young woman. Her skin was brown, and she was dressed in a navy skirt and a white blouse; her long, kinky hair was twisted high on top of her head. When she saw Pascal, she hurried to the door.

"Oh, isn't it wonderful," she said. "Miss Anderson and I just arrived and already we have students. I'm Miss Harris. Pleased to know you." She shook hands.

Miss Anderson clung to her broom. She seemed afraid to stand near them. Pascal wondered what to think.

Chapter Ten

Miss Anderson licked her thin lips and said, "Miss Harris is sent down here by the American Missionary Association."

Pascal watched Miss Anderson tremble. She stared at them as if she hadn't seen many colored people. He was surprised at how bold he felt, how different from just two weeks before. His feet were sore from walking, but his heart was healing.

"Welcome," said Miss Harris, smiling. "Won't you step in?" She moved aside to wave them in the door.

The schoolroom was small with white plastered walls, plank wooden floors, and the smell of soap. A round wood-burning stove squatted in the center. Five chairs of assorted sizes and a rocker with one arm stood shyly side by side. A kitchen table faced the chairs.

"As you can see," said Miss Anderson,

waving, "conditions are primitive." To Pascal, the room looked like a king's palace.

While they stood in the schoolroom shifting feet, Miss Harris hurried to drag a leather trunk from the back room. Mr. Freedman helped her. She lifted two brass clasps and threw open the top.

"We have slates and chalk and primers," she said, lifting a writing slate.

"Don't let them touch it," said Miss Anderson. Her voice grew shrill. "They'll break something."

"I'm just showing them," Miss Harris told her. "Shall we learn something now?"

"Dear Miss Harris," said Miss Anderson, "I think the crippled child should go home and dress for school. We can't have you ragged," she told Pascal, pointing to his torn-off pants.

"I have another shirt," he said, "but I don't have no other pants." There it was again, he thought. She had called him "crippled child." That was what everyone saw about him first, his crippled leg and weak, twisted hand. But he was a boy with a family farm. His name was on the paper!

"Well," said Miss Anderson, "buy another pair of pants."

"We don't have enough money, ma'am." This lady didn't seem to understand. Just then Judith Bibb burst through the door followed by her brothers and little sister, and then by her parents.

"School," called Judith. "Can I come to school, ma'am?"

"You should say, 'Good afternoon' and 'May I,'" Miss Anderson told her, and she shook her head at Miss Harris.

"Welcome," called Miss Harris. Her smile showed a broad gap between her two front teeth. "Of course you can attend school. At least until a separate school is opened for you."

Miss Anderson folded her arms tightly. "There are those who fear the mixing of the colored and white races," she said.

Pascal wondered what that meant.

"However," Miss Anderson said, "I will telegraph for orders, and until we have orders, you may attend school here."

The afternoon sun warmed Pascal's back; prospects of school-learning burned in his heart. Now he could be a smart landowner; they wouldn't lose their farm like some poor white folks did. He could feel his back straighten. Forty acres of land and a school to attend! Wouldn't Mama be pleased?

The City and Bibb families finally decided they would return for school in two days. Mrs. Bibb said, "We have to find our new land and get settled. I'm very very very anxious to see the light of it, you know."

Glancing down, Miss Anderson stared at her tan apron. She quickly slipped it off and folded it twice over her arm.

"We'll be looking forward to seeing you," said Miss Harris. "I know how it is at planting time." She smiled her gap-toothed smile. "And," she said, "if grown people can't come during the day, they can attend in the evening. Miss Anderson and I will alternate in teaching night school for adults."

Clasping her hands behind her back, she added, "By the way, every Friday night the Union League will hold a meeting here to discuss Republican politics. Everyone is invited."

"Yes," said Miss Anderson. "This storefront is rented by the Union League clubs of New York." She pressed her lips together.

Mrs. Bibb said, "Our children never got no school-learning. I'm so very very very pleased we came to Georgia." As she spoke, baby Daniel spit white milk down the back of her dark blue dress.

"Weren't no public schools in the South nowhere we been," said Judith. "Now we going to a real schoolhouse." She stroked the door frame and rested her cheek against it.

Pascal glanced down the street where a

long line of people waited at the Freedmen's Bureau. He saw three riders galloping toward that line, pistols held skyward. "Look back there," he yelled, pointing.

The riders fired into the office, fired into the crowd. Pascal saw the two Bureau workers on hands and knees under their outdoor table. No wonder they had been nervous. He heard people screaming; saw children scattering across the street. One horse raced away, dragging its wagon turned on the side.

Miss Harris was quick. "Down!" she called, and stooped inside the doorway. Pascal pulled Gideon and Nelly down, and the others stooped. The riders galloped toward them.

One after the other, the three men fired into the schoolhouse. Glass shattered and fell tinkling. Pungent gun smoke burned Pascal's eyes.

"Go home, you Yankees," called one rider to the teachers. "Go home facefirst or we'll send you back in coffins feetfirst."

Chapter Eleven

Pascal helped trembling Miss Anderson to her feet. Miss Harris stood picking glass out of her skirt. In spite of the shooting, they seemed calm. Pascal wished he could tell them how thankful he was that they were there. Gratitude burned like fire in his heart. What brave women they were to come to the angry South to teach former slaves.

He found out that no one had been killed, and that the town had a doctor willing to treat the wounded colored people. Since they weren't needed to help, the City family hurried away.

In a low voice, Mr. Freedman said, "Confederate soldiers might come and shoot up your farm, Gideon. You still want it?" Pascal had wondered about that.

"I'll farm my land," said Gideon. "If they shoot me dead, I'll have a place for my grave."

Pascal moaned. What choice did they have? How could they make a living except on their family farm?

He spotted a tan pebble that was almost round. Would it give them luck? Whispering, "Pick a pretty pebble," he tucked it in his pocket.

"Want to play 'Shadow, shadow on the road'?" asked Nelly.

"How we play it?"

"Look," she said. Their shadows were in front of them. Glancing up, Nelly said, "Keep watching. Call, 'Shadow, shadow, change'!"

As Nelly called, her shadow moved from her back to her side. "The road just turned," Pascal said. He laughed.

When they arrived at the cave, Gideon held up the paper. "Here's our title to forty acres between a lake and a creek." His voice was low, and he wet his lips.

Suddenly Pascal realized that none of them knew what their land was like. He stared downhill. What if they had to cut down a forest of trees?

He stared at the ground. Next in his mind he saw a stinking swamp, bubbling gas through ooze, and set between a lake and a creek. How could they farm a swamp?

Mr. Freedman cleared his throat. "Well, tomorrow morning we men should go find

Gideon City's forty acres."

Pascal and Nelly glanced at each other. "We all should go," said Pascal. Gladness nodded.

"All the City family," said Nelly. Pascal smiled. Come fair weather or foul, he had family!

The next morning Gideon led them uphill. He had directions from the Freedmen's Bureau, and they were almost halfway there already. About three more miles to go.

On the way a smiling man and woman walked up. The woman carried an infant; the man held a toddler's hand. "Y'all seen Wilson Road?" the man asked. The City family said no, but Pascal looked at their map and title and pointed out the possible direction.

Another younger man with his wife on a one-eyed mule asked, "Y'all heard of Elmwood Lane?" They had three children.

"No," said Gideon. "We be looking for Ghost Tree Lane."

"I sure hope y'all find y'all farm," the woman called.

A man with a white beard was walking with what seemed to be his redheaded son and a daughter-in-law. "We're looking for the Land Bureau," he said. Gideon pointed the way to River Stop.

"Poor folks white and black be getting land," said Gideon. Pascal nodded. How wonderful that poor people could farm on their own land.

They passed several crossroads and four abandoned chicken-scratch farms. With each step Pascal's heart sank. The woodlands and meadows seemed to have more and more rocks and boulders. Would the land be so rocky nothing would grow?

"Gideon," he said, "maybe freedom be about more than land."

Gideon was silent. "Never you mind," he said after a while. "I ain't crying over poor land."

Nodding, Mr. Freedman said, "I seen a heap of fair farms on failed farmland." He cleared his throat.

A wagon drew near, and children cheered. Pascal waved as the Bibbs drove past them. Mr. Bibb sat in the back of the wagon with Mark on his lap. Mrs. Bibb held the reins up front; Naomi and Judith, holding the baby, sat beside her. Pascal watched Judith wave the baby's blanket until the Bibbs turned a bend in the road and Pascal couldn't see them anymore.

Mr. Freedman said, "I wonder what kind of farmland they give white people?" Raising his eyebrows, he grunted.

Gideon looked at the drawing, read the directions, and they walked another half mile. He pointed. "The creek starts here."

A rocky creek flowed across the road. Planks showed where there had been a bridge, probably before the war, but the sandy creek was shallow. A recent wagon had rolled across without getting bogged down. Gideon took off his boots. Nelly and Gladness raised long skirts, and they all waded across. Gideon walked on, staring at his feet, afraid, it seemed, to look up.

"The Ghost Tree," called Pascal. He couldn't miss it. A huge lone oak stood guard back from the road. Rain had washed the soil from its roots until they looked like raised chicken feet.

"Bear den," Mr. Freedman said, pointing to the cavern under the tree's roots. "I bet bears sleep there all winter, and foxes raise young there in spring."

They walked farther, and Pascal turned to face the land. "Y'all, I can see a shining of the lake over yonder," he said. "This be it."

He turned to see tears on his brother's face. Tears welled up in Pascal's eyes as well. Running to Gideon, Pascal buried his face in his brother's side, hugging him before turning around.

This was the prettiest land Pascal had ever

seen. Besides the Ghost Tree, there were maybe thirty other trees, mostly wind-dancing willows, scattered along the edges of the lake and the creek.

Otherwise grass and wildflowers blanketed the land. Meadowlarks flashed yellow feathers, singing as they flew across the flowers. Red-winged blackbirds called from cat-nine-tails at the creek. The land smelled clean and fertile and good.

"We need to plow the grass under for planting crops," Gideon said softly, "but we got no mule and no plow."

Mr. Freedman held up his hand. "If you plow, the first wind blows the good topsoil away. But Indians out West do different: They set fire. We got a lake, we got a creek. We wet down the trees and outer area and we burn the grass."

"Burn the land?" asked Gideon.

"Yes, sir," said Mr. Freedman. "Set fire and control it. Enough dry grass in there still. That leaves fertile land all freed up for farming."

Pascal said, "We got five hoes and some bags of seed for cotton; besides that, we got seeds for potatoes, turnips, salad, beans, and squashes. Even watermelon."

Mr. Freedman waved toward the land. "After we burn away the grass, we dig holes, plant seeds, and cover them. That's all. No plow needed. But, we'll need help. Plenty colored folks on the road we can ask for help. And I can make more hoes."

"Sure is fine looking," said Gladness. Suddenly she squealed and ran into the waist-high wildflowers. "Flowers," she screamed, "pink and yellow and blue and white." She turned. "Can we leave some of them?" Arms raised, she swirled her long skirt. Nelly, laughing, ran into the wildflowers after her.

Mr. Freedman followed Gladness onto the land. "Where do you want your house, Gideon?"

"House?" Gideon covered his face with a hand. "We ain't got no money for a house."

"I'll plant a food garden right by the back door of the house," said Gladness, ignoring Gideon's words. "Them seeds for vegetables and watermelon, they be ours to grow. Mine and Nelly's."

The grass was elbow-high to Pascal. He waded over to the mighty oak. "I wonder why it be called Ghost Tree?" he asked.

Only low grass grew in the shade of the huge oak. Black branches jutted out from the tree trunk like witch's arms with bony fingers. The tree had mighty limbs on all sides. Its trunk was so big it would take three men to reach hands around it. And it was bent to the east, then straightened to the west. Looking up from under the tree, Pascal was filled with wonder.

He thought about the tree on the plantation where the overseer whipped slaves. Pascal had had to stretch his arms around that tree, and the man had switched his bare back with hickory sticks. Pascal gritted his teeth. How had he lived through that?

"How about here for the house?" shouted Mr. Freedman. He stood on a little hilltop. "It overlooks the farm. I can see the lake, the road, the creek, and clear back to the pines."

Pascal limped up to where Mr. Freedman stood, arms outstretched. When Gideon reached there, tears flowed again. Gideon said, "It can't be the truth. I will not hold this farm to my heart and lose my heart in pain." He shook his head.

Nelly and Gladness ran up the rise.

Taking the paper from his brother, Pascal read the directions slowly. "These be your forty acres, all right," he called. "Walls of Jericho!" Pascal slapped his brother's back. "Believe it," he called, laughing and crying at the same time.

"And we'll have a pretty little house on this land in no time," said Mr. Freedman, rubbing his hands and smiling. "I got it all worked out in my head."

Chapter Twelve

Keeping a road-front of April wildflowers for Gladness, the three men — Gideon, Mr. Freedman, and Pascal — set fire to the meadow. Pascal was amazed at how easy it was. The blackened earth smoldered for two days while they planed the fields.

"When I was with the army, I worked for my food and pay," Gideon told Pascal. "Now that I be a boss man, it be my turn to hire others."

"Y'all want to work?" he asked two people passing on the road.

"You paying?" the man asked.

"Three meals a day and a willow tree to sleep under," said Gideon. "When my cotton crop comes in, I be paying in money."

"Good enough for me," the man called, and his wife joined him. Others also accepted the terms happily.

"First time ever I worked for a colored

boss man," said one woman. "First time, and I like it."

For two weeks, with extra workers they marked rows, measured off spaces, planted cotton, and watered the seeds.

A Union soldier wearing a red bandanna stared when Gideon offered him work. "I be not much of a farmer," the man said, "but I can cook. Y'all be needing a good cook."

The soldier's name was Emmanuel; medium tall, with dark brown skin, he had a beard and graying bushy hair. For meat in his meals he hunted quail and wild turkey, and he fished in streams. Gladness was freed from cooking so that she could farm.

Pascal noticed that on some days Mr. Freedman would disappear for hours, wading jauntily across the creek and trotting out the road they had come along. In the evening he would return smiling like a cat that's been licking cow cream.

Three days a week Pascal, Nelly, and Gladness left in early morning to walk to school, taking shortcuts through farmland. Pascal expected to see Judith Bibb and her brothers, but they never came. After walking back, Pascal and the others worked chopping cotton, tending the field.

Pascal thought, now that I be a landowner, I be somebody! But was that true?

What had really changed? He felt different, but was it the forty acres that made the difference? If not, what was it?

Besides working on the farm, and disappearing sometimes, Mr. Freedman repaired porch steps, nailed window frames, and replaced wagon sides in River Stop to earn money. With it he bought flour and sugar and coffee for their meals.

Gladness and Nelly bought ribbons with his pennies. They loved to tie pretty colors around their necks and to braid colorful ribbons in their hair. Nelly told Pascal, "I be so happy Miss Gladness came with us. Now, I not the only girl in the family."

Emmanuel baked biscuits every morning, true to Gideon's promise. For an oven he used a stone pit he had built. They all enjoyed Emmanuel's soft biscuits for breakfast; his meat stews or fish frys for dinner at noon; and another stew or quail for supper in the evening.

Gideon was fascinated by the Ghost Tree. "No one calls a tree a Ghost Tree without there's a reason," he told Pascal.

One evening he decided to study his tree, so he slid down under the roots. In seconds he crawled out, howling in pain.

"What be the matter?" called Gladness,

running over. Everyone ran after her.

Gideon slapped his face and arms and legs. "Fleas," he screamed, dancing and howling. "I be set on fire from bites!"

"Hurry to the creek," called Gladness. "Cold water will ease them bites." On hands and knees she searched among the wildflowers for medicine.

Scratching his bites, Gideon lay in the cool creek. Gladness was quick to choose wide green leaves of a low plant. At the creek she hammered the leaves with stones from the creek bed. "Here," she said, "rub these on all the bites to draw the poison out."

Gideon sat up and plastered his face and arms and legs with the leaves. "Ooh," he told Pascal, who squatted by the water. "This be better than the balm of Gilead. Gladness be a healer, all right."

Mr. Freedman called, "I know how to clear them fleas out." As Nelly and Pascal watched, he shoveled embers from the cooking fire into the hole under the raised roots. Leaves in the cavern smoldered. "I told you that animals slept there," he said as he lifted the shovel. "Proved me right. Smoke will clear them fleas out."

After that Gideon and Gladness sat under the Ghost Tree almost every evening. Pascal liked the happy murmur of their voices.

They would talk until a million friendly stars came twinkling to join them.

Evenings Nelly and Pascal played hide-and-go-seek along the creek among the willow trees. One night Nelly cried, "Oh, the mystery lights are out." She began to run and skip.

"You mean the fireflies?" asked Pascal.

"Come dance with me, Pascal. Dance around a mystery light. Follow it. When the light goes out, you hold your breath until it comes on again. Then you make a wish."

He limped, following her.

"Do you feel the mystery?"

"Nooo, no. Maybe. Yesss? What mystery?"

Nelly waved her arms and danced. "The mystery of wishes."

"They're just bugs, you know. Do your wishes come true?"

Nelly put her hands on her hips. "Pascal, ain't this a wish come true? *We living out the dream of every slave what ever been borned.* Landowners of the prettiest farm on God's green earth!"

One day in May, Mr. Freedman began digging a trench in a square on the hilltop and filling it with stones. For a week he worked at digging a shaft from the center of the hilltop down to the bottom of the hill. Emmanuel used some of the topsoil for a second food garden that would ripen later.

Pascal asked, "Why the hole, Mister Freedman?"

"Escape, Pascal," he said. "I ain't building no house for colored people that don't have as many ways to escape as there be people inside."

On rainy days Pascal and Nelly played sliding down the tunnel. Pascal slid feetfirst, but Nelly dived in headfirst. They smoothed the walls and let high grass and wildflowers hide the outside entrance. They could use it to escape, all right.

But the thought of having to escape frightened Pascal. Would something go wrong? Surely if they did everything right, they could farm in peace?

In late May, Mr. Freedman asked for help: "I need the hired men and Gideon. My apologies to the ladies. Pascal, we need you to guide us so nobody breaks an ankle."

Hands on hips, Nelly stood with the hired women and watched them leave. Gladness waved, and Pascal waved back.

When they reached old farms some miles away, they saw that Mr. Freedman had separated sides from several abandoned houses.

Walls had been nailed firm and were ready to carry; he even had a roof lying waiting.

"A house all built," said Gideon. "All it needs is putting together." He covered his face.

"Well," said Mr. Freedman, "don't just stand there. Let's march."

Trip after trip, men carried house walls and propped them on the stone foundation in the trenches. After each trip Pascal grew more excited and happy.

After a week of heavy work the sides were in place, but Pascal worried. As he and Nelly stood on the hilltop, he pointed to the walls.

"Don't none of them meet," he told her.

"Mister Freedman must have him a plan," she said.

"You right," said Mr. Freedman, walking up behind them.

On the last trip they carried narrow wood sections. Mr. Freedman fit doors on all four corners of the house. Now the home was eight-sided, and the aged wood shone like silver.

But the roof stuck out over the front. They were standing by the house when Pascal asked, "Why does the roof hang over?"

Mr. Freedman said, "Ain't you never heard of a porch?"

Gideon gasped.

Pascal swallowed hard. "This be the prettiest little house I ever did see," he told Mr. Freedman. They not only had a family farm, but they had a family farm with a farmhouse!

"It looks pretty enough to be angel Michael's house in heaven," said Nelly. She stroked the wall of the farmhouse, then hugged a corner with her arms stretched wide.

Pascal's heart felt squeezed for joy every time he walked around their home. In good weather boys and men slept outside while Gladness, Nelly, and the hired women slept in the house. On rainy nights everyone slept inside on the dirt floor. Mr. Freedman promised to let them build furniture during the winter.

Nelly tied grass on a stick to make a broom and swept the floor daily. More than once Pascal saw his brother walking around the farmhouse, touching the walls and smiling. Pascal couldn't look up at their home on the hillside without smiling himself. Sometimes he felt so happy, he wondered if he had died and gone to heaven.

Gideon was right, Pascal thought. People looked at them differently when they saw the farmhouse and the cotton fields. Sometimes white people rode by in carriages and stared at their farm. Pascal's heart swelled with pride. The City family was looked upon with respect.

A lame-leg, twisted-hand boy who owned land was somebody.

Onc day Mr. Freedman said, "Now we need logs to make the porch columns. I found four in matching size. Trouble is, they be rooted in the ground and pine-branched to the sky."

"I got me a hatchet," one hired man said. The next morning a few men left with Gideon and Mr. Freedman to cut porch columns.

Morning mist burned in the joyful sunshine of June. Golden meadowlarks flew by singing, and a breeze rippled wildflowers and grass. Somewhere a woodpecker nailed *tat-tat, tat-tat* on a tree trunk. In the field seven hired women, Nelly, and Gladness bent over with tin cans, watering the cotton.

That June morning Pascal decided not to work. Nobody was watching him; his brother and the other men were gone. He would sneak away and go looking for the Bibbs's farm. He searched for hours, wandering in one direction, then another. Far back in a field of grass he finally saw their wagon covered with a canvas tent top.

"How to do, Bibbs?" he called as he limped toward them.

Matthew peeped out of the wagon like a

shy squirrel from a tree hole. He pulled back. Slowly Judith climbed out and held up a hand. "Ma says don't come no farther," she said in a weak voice. "We don't want you to catch no disease."

Her voice quivered. "We all been sick. Mark and baby Daniel are dead, stinking, and ain't even been buried yet."

"Dead?" called Pascal. "What happened?" Two children dead? He stepped back and clutched his forehead. His heart began to pound, and he held his breath.

"Pa had typhoid first. He was lying low and likely to die. Then Mark, Daniel, Ma, and me were struck with fever, red spots, vomiting, and loose bowels. Now there's only three children. Pa is weak, but he's alive."

Pascal called, "Wait right there. I'll get help."

Judith pointed. "Go back this short way. We're your neighbors right across the lake from you. We saw your fire."

Mrs. Bibb looked out the tent flap. "Pascal," she called weakly, "the good Lord must have sent you. Our food gave out last week. We are very very very much suffering for the wants of something to eat."

"I'll be right back," Pascal called and, heart pounding, he began running.

Chapter Thirteen

As Gideon, Mr. Freedman, and the others followed him, Pascal said, "The Bibbs live right on the other side of our lake. They ain't planted none 'cause they been sick enough to die." No one had asked him why he skipped tending cotton that day.

When they reached the Bibbs's wagon, Emmanuel made a fire and began heating food for everyone to eat together. From the army he knew about typhoid fever, and he said it was safe.

Mrs. Bibb's hands were trembling as she spooned quail stew to her mouth. "Thank you very very very much, and may the Lord bless you all," she said. Mr. Bibb sat against the wagon wheel to eat.

Pascal said, "Here, I'll help you," and spoon-fed Judith, Matthew, and Naomi. He felt good feeding his hungry friends. Nelly held the bowl for Pascal. Little Naomi lay across her mother's knees, too weak to sit.

Nelly nudged Pascal. "Remember when they fed us corn mush?"

After supper, Mr. Freedman stood. "We men can help you bury the boys," he said softly. Gideon began to dig near their wagon.

Mrs. Bibb said, "Only one grave. I want our sons to keep each other company till Resurrection Day." The hired men took turns shoveling until the hole was deep enough.

Mr. Bibb, too weak to stand, knelt by the grave and read from the Bible over his dead sons. " 'The Lord giveth and the Lord taketh away,' " he read, " 'blessed be the name of the Lord.' "

For a week in June Emmanuel cooked at the Bibbs's farm, and everyone ate meals together there. On the last evening of the week, Mr. Bibb said, "Your cotton looks good. Could you help us clear our field? I feel right bad about being weak." They were sitting around Emmanuel's cooking fire.

"Never you mind," said Gideon. "You been mighty sick." He sniffed the air. "I smell rain."

Mr. Freedman pointed. "Those be rain clouds in the west, and no wind."

"Yes," said Gideon, standing. "No better

time than now. We'll start the fire from all four sides and down the center. We pray it finishes burning before the rain."

As their farmland rose up in flames, Matthew and little Naomi hid from the smoky roar. However, a brave, blinking Judith skipped nervously, helping Pascal and Nelly wet down the field near their wagon. They used water from the lake.

"Where we lived before in Tennessee we had a spring," said Judith. "We used to bathe in the spring."

Pascal asked, "Was that where or when?"

Nelly and Judith laughed. "Get on, Pascal," said Nelly.

By midnight, when they had a thunderstorm, the Bibbs's field had been burned flat and was ready for planting.

By mid-June everyone on the City family's farm was learning to read. One night Pascal heard Gladness tell her grandfather, "This here letter be called a *K*. See the leg and arm kick?" Mr. Freedman repeated, "*K*," learning his letters. Gideon read everything Pascal brought home, and he was teaching some of the hired men and women.

By July Judith and Matthew were strong enough to attend school. "I can hardly wait for my first day at school!" Judith said the evening before. Head down, Matthew stood at a distance listening to Nelly, Pascal, and Judith talk under the Ghost Tree.

Nelly skipped in a circle. "I can count to a thousand already, and read little words."

"I copy sayings and poetry, a few words at a time, in a box with dirt on the bottom. Fifteen minutes each day, I write words," said Pascal. "Sometimes in the mornings, there be about sixty children and ten or twelve grown-ups for Miss Harris and Miss Anderson to teach. Then they take turns teaching night school just for grown-ups."

That warm summer night Nelly led the children to run after fireflies, and they all made wishes. When Mr. Bibb rang a bell, the Bibb children walked home.

The next morning Judith and Matthew Bibb walked to school with Nelly, Gladness, and Pascal. On the way a farmer named Mr. Alonzo Deliverance waved to them. He had milked his cows in darkness and now he led them to pasture.

"How's your cotton?" he called to Pascal.

"Fair to middling, sir. How're your cows?"

"Fair to middling. Got customers in River Stop buying my Sherman Lands milk. They tell me there're thousands of farmers like us after slavery. Glory, glory, glory, hallelujah!"

"Amen!" called Gladness. They waved good-bye.

"Y'all know that cows don't give milk?" said Pascal.

"Sure enough they do," Judith said, nodding.

No," he said, "you gotta take it from them." The girls moaned. "And, y'all know why cows wear bells?"

"Nooo," said Nelly, smiling.

"'Cause they can't blow their horns."

"Aw, Pascal," Nelly said as they laughed.

Pascal sniffed the good smell of cow manure. Maybe they should ask for some for their gardens?

After they passed Mr. Deliverance, Nelly told Judith and Matthew, "Miss Anderson believes in hitting with her ruler. She don't mean no harm, though."

"I learned my letters real quick," said Gladness. "Pascal here helped me. Now I be reading in a primer. In numbers, I be adding and subtracting. Me and Nelly finished object counting." She pointed to Pascal. "He be in fifth reader and doing fractions."

Judith asked, "Pascal, how did you learn to read and cipher?"

"For five or so years," Pascal said, "Master's mother taught me reading, writing, and arithmetic. As her eyes been failing, I read to her from *Harper's Weekly* magazine and I read her Whitman's poetry. But it all be a secret, 'cause you remember it be against the law to teach a slave to read or write."

He groaned. "One day she up and went to glory. With her gone, I was back to running errands and shooing flies." He shook his head and frowned at the memory. But now he had a family, and he was landowner of a family farm. He smiled; life had changed.

When they reached the storefront school, about fifty students, colored and white, stood outside the door. Pascal saw a lantern glowing inside. He whispered to Matthew and Judith, "Before you walk in, Miss Anderson makes boys bow, girls curtsy, and you say, 'Good morning, Miss Anderson. Good morning, Miss Harris.'"

At the door Matthew murmured his greeting, but Miss Anderson caught him by the ear. She made him repeat "Good morning" until he spoke loudly. Inside, the students sat in chairs or on the floor and did their assignments.

With a finger Pascal added fractions in clay dust in a box. Miss Harris looked over his shoulder. "That one's right." Sitting cross-legged on the floor, he smoothed the dirt and began the second fraction. Miss Harris whispered, "She gives dumb white children slates to write on, but a smart colored student like you has to use a dirt box. It just isn't fair."

"That be all right, ma'am," Pascal whispered back.

She patted his shoulder. "Good for you. Don't let anyone keep you back, Pascal!"

"Yes, ma'am." Pascal looked around. Nelly and Gladness sat side by side, adding. Judith was sitting on the floor, copying letters on her slate and making the sounds. She'd learn fast.

Their hours of school passed rapidly. As they left, Miss Harris followed them to the door. "Gladness, there's a big Union League meeting here in two weeks to select candidates for office. We'll elect good people. Negroes are fifty percent of the citizens of Georgia." She smiled at Pascal. "That's what fraction, Pascal?"

"One half, ma'am."

"Bring all the City family, and you Bibbs tell your parents to come."

Pascal limped away, thinking that being smart and owning land could definitely make up for having a crooked leg and a weak hand.

Chapter Fourteen

In July Judith and her brother missed school for two days. Pascal worried about them. After setting his hoe upright the next day, he glanced around. No one seemed to notice him, not even Nelly. He would sneak away. Nelly might think he'd gone for a drink of water.

Farming in the hot summer sun was hard work. Pascal wasn't used to it; he had always worked at the Big House. Chopping cotton hurt his arms, his shoulders, his back, his legs. It hurt so much that sometimes he hated that family farm; but right away he would feel guilty.

Sometimes, he would lie down in the rows. Today, he just sneaked away. Taking the long way to avoid being caught, he walked to find Judith. He finally reached the Bibbs's farm.

Mr. Bibb looked out of their wagon.

"Praise the Lord, Pascal. If you're looking for Judith, she's working in the field, watering crops with her ma."

"Thank you, sir," said Pascal. "Tonight's the Union League meeting. Are y'all going?"

"I'd like to go, but today I had to take my horses to be shod. I found a colored blacksmith over yonder in Jubilee Town. All colored people. Barbershop, blacksmith shop, grocery store — everything over there. Even a hospital with a doctor and a nurse. Could of helped us with the typhoid." He shook his head sadly. "Anyway, I'm plumb tuckered out."

News of people in Jubilee Town was good. Pascal had heard about them. He wondered if it was safer living with all colored people in a town, or safer to be mixed with whites along a road. He said good-bye and walked slowly under that blazing sun. When he reached the lake, he discovered Judith hiding behind a willow watching for him.

"Pascal," she said, eyes wide, "there's trouble brewing. I saw men arresting colored people on the road."

Pascal shrugged. "We ain't done nothing wrong. Why weren't you in school yesterday?"

She picked up the hem of her long skirt and twisted it. "Last time, Miss Anderson let me scribe wet clay. I wrote 'Love Ma,' 'Love Pa' on it."

"I remember. You write nice letters."

"But, Pascal," she said, "when I brought it home, Ma held it upside down and said, 'How very very very nice.' And then Pa went to Ma and he held it upside down, too." She stomped her foot. "All those years Pa read to us out of the Bible, and it was just a big lie. He has it memorized."

"So, they don't know how to read," Pascal said, shrugging. "There ain't no shame in that."

"There is!" She stomped her foot again. "I don't want to know more than my own ma and pa!" She began crying.

"But, Judith, you gotta. You gotta make sure you don't lose your farm. And your children'll have a mother who can read. Don't you see?"

Judith wiped her eyes. "Oh, all right. Maybe I'll go back." She brushed her skirt. "Anyway, be sure and get a piece of paper that keeps them from arresting colored people. The men didn't stop no white people."

Pascal strolled through waves of heat to return. He was eager to go to the Union League meeting. From tooth to toenail he felt himself a Republican. Those Reconstruction plans were so wonderful they made gooseflesh rise on his arms. They really helped poor people, colored and white.

When he reached home, he found Gideon digging under the Ghost Tree with his army shovel. His brother hadn't missed him in the cotton row. Pascal knelt by a root. "You fixing to bury someone?" he asked.

Gideon leaned on the shovel. "Pascal," he said, "this here Ghost Tree be a mystery." He pulled his little brother into the cool dirt cavern below the roots. "See here?"

Pascal saw that someone had hacked a space into a huge root. "Why?" he asked.

"I don't rightly know," said Gideon. "I reckon it was once hidden under dirt, but rains washed it clear."

"So," whispered Pascal, "you figure someone hid something down here? Master once found silverware and candlesticks someone had buried on his land."

Gideon nodded. "I be about to find whatever it be," he said, putting his finger to his lips. "Don't tell."

Before returning to his cotton row, Pascal held on to a root and threw back his head. Wonder overcame him whenever he looked through the mighty oak's branches that reached for the sky with leafy green fingers.

After supper they gathered to walk toward town. Jasmine growing roadside scented the air with excitement. It was an evening for Pascal to float on summer's hot breath. This was the first time they had all left the farm to go any farther than around the lake. As they started, Gideon kept glancing over his shoulder.

"I hear there be people riding in the night and ruining colored people's farms," he said. Pascal stared at him. Would that happen to their farm?

"You hear all kinds of things," said Mr. Freedman. "There be colored folks what can't stop complaining. Over in that Jubilee Town they lose sleep watching their land. Afraid some night rider will come pull up their cotton, I suppose." He chuckled.

"Wait up," Pascal said suddenly. "I want to tell the Bibbs something." Two hired women hadn't joined them yet, anyway, and he had an idea. He couldn't allow their farm to be ruined.

Limping and skipping, he ran to the Bibbs's farm. Judith and Matthew walked to meet him.

"Judith," he said, panting, "will you and Matthew play over by our farm? Just so folks think . . . well, think that y'all live there."

"To keep it safe from the night riders?" she asked.

Pascal nodded. "But don't tell nobody, hear? I don't want Gideon or Nelly to worry."

Already white people passing their farm had stared to see Nelly and Pascal playing with the Bibbs under the Ghost Tree. Once, Pascal heard a woman ask, "Is that a colored people's farm? Or white?"

And the woman riding beside her had said, "White. Look how well it's cultivated. Colored people must be working for them."

Pascal had been angry. He had wanted to tell those women that that was his brother Gideon's forty acres. But now he thought, maybe if white folks don't know, they won't ruin our crops.

"Anyway," he told Judith and Matthew, "thank you."

When Pascal returned, Gideon was saying, "Farms are suffering for the want of water, too. Ain't rained in a month. Our creek is low."

He sounds like a regular farmer worrying about rain, thought Pascal. We be a farm family all right. "Reminds me," he said, "y'all know the difference between a rainy day and a person with a terrible toothache?"

"What?" Nelly asked.

"One be pouring with rain," he said, "and the other be roaring with pain."

Gideon groaned.

Nelly said, "Get on, Pascal." She pointed to a firefly and ran to follow it and make a wish. Swinging his walking stick, Pascal remained with the men.

Mr. Freedman said, "Now that we've finished the porch, we should think about digging a well." He added, "We bought whitewash, but painting inside can wait until after harvest."

Pascal smiled. That front porch on the farmhouse was like heaven on earth. Evenings they sat on the porch watching stars blinking in the sky. Everybody had a favorite spot to sit. Mr. Freedman and a hired man argued over how they were going to make furniture in the winter. Next summer they figured to have rockers on the front porch.

A hired man said, "Some farmers be worried over boll weevils and army worms eating their crops. We don't have us none."

"I think burning our earth killed them off," said Gideon.

"No," Nelly called. "Them boll weevils wouldn't dare set feets on your land. They be too scared of a whipping at the tree."

They all laughed, and Pascal remembered how they used to talk about the farm.

"We'll be picking cotton beginning in August," said Gideon.

Pascal's heart flipped like a pancake on a griddle. When they sold their cotton, they'd be rich. Lately he had looked in store windows in River Stop. He had never bought anything in all his life, but now they would have money. Maybe he could buy pants and a shirt that fit him! Walls of Jericho! Wouldn't that be grand? He skipped a step as they trudged on the road.

Maybe freedom was wearing nice clothes and having people look at you with respect? He kept wondering about that. He was sorry Mama didn't live to see this day.

When they reached Main Street, two hundred or more colored people were milling around. Pascal stared at all the young men. One of his brothers might be among them. He searched for anyone who looked like them. When he saw thin dark men, he walked over and said, "I be looking for three brothers. My mama's name was Jerusalem City, and we come from South Carolina."

Men shook their heads and patted his back. "Sorry, son."

He wasn't the only one looking for family.

125

It seemed half the people there were asking if anyone knew a family member sold away in slavery.

A white man waved to the City family. "Y'all get your work contracts before you go to the meeting," he called, pointing to men writing at tables.

"That must be the piece of paper Judith told me about," Pascal said, clutching his stick. They joined a line of people.

"What paper?" asked Gideon. Gladness and Mr. Freedman glanced at each other. Her hand held her throat.

"It's all right," the man said, putting a thumb under his suspender strap and walking over to them. "There's new Black Codes in the South. Any colored people found without work contracts can be arrested for vagrancy. Then they assign them to a plantation to work for a year."

"Do they get paid?" asked Mr. Freedman.

"No, that's their fine for vagrancy. They work a year without wages. But don't worry, y'all on Sherman Land. We'll make out your contracts. It's just for the lazy Negroes wandering the roads."

"Lazy?" said Pascal. "They ain't lazy. They be looking for lost family, or looking for pay!" He felt hot in the face. Of course, those people weren't landowners like him,

126

but they were still people. Weren't they?

Ignoring him, the man told others behind the City family, "If y'all ain't working now, we'll set you up on a farm. Step right up for contract papers." He walked over to newcomers and repeated his message.

"That be slavery all over again," Gideon said. He stared at the man's back with fiery eyes. "I ain't signing no work contract. I'll tell them white masters what I think of their Black Codes."

Pascal held his stomach. This time it was more like a knife than a fist that pained his gut.

Chapter Fifteen

In the dark under a clear, moonless sky, people stepped up to a table and agreed to a work contract. A white man wrote while moths sizzled flying into the flames of his lantern.

Gladness's work contract read:

SAID GLADNESS CITY AGREES TO WORK FOR SAID GIDEON CITY FOR ONE YEAR FROM THE FOURTEENTH DAY OF JULY 1865 UNTIL THE FOURTEENTH DAY OF JULY 1866, AT ANY KIND OF LABOR SAID GIDEON CITY DIRECTS, AND AGREES TO SERVE HIM FAITHFULLY AND CONSTANTLY.

IF SUCH LABOR BE FAITHFULLY PERFORMED, SAID GIDEON CITY ON HIS PART AGREES TO FURNISH QUARTERS AND FOOD, AND TO PAY TWENTY-FOUR DOLLARS AT END OF ONE YEAR'S SERVICE.

SHOULD SAID GLADNESS CITY BE

INSOLENT, IMPUDENT, OR SASSY TO
GIDEON CITY, OR BE IDLE OR SICK MORE
THAN TWO DAYS, SHE IS SUBJECT TO DIS-
CHARGE AND SHALL FORFEIT ALL RIGHTS
BETWEEN PARTIES. SIGNED IN PRESENCE
OF:

And the man wrote his own name.
Gladness signed her name.

Gideon was breathing in hot gasps. Pascal
kept whispering, "It's all right, Gideon. Our
contracts be to you. Think of the people who
gotta work for the white masters again."

Gideon's turn came. Pascal squeezed his
arm.

"Your name?"

"Gideon City."

The man stared at his paper, then stared
up at Gideon. He frowned and wrote:
*Gideon City has title to Sherman Land —
Forty Acres.* Pascal tugged his brother's arm.
When Gideon took the paper and walked
away without saying anything, Pascal almost
fainted in relief.

Two people in a line beside them began to
wail. They called, "But we be here for the
Union Club's meeting."

"Sorry, y'all just signed a work contract
with Mister Howard, and your work begins
now," the man said.

Mr. Howard swaggered over, carrying a

rifle in both hands. "Are y'all being impudent?" he asked.

"No, sir," the man said. He and the woman looked down.

"Well, then, y'all climb into the back of that wagon."

Pascal moaned. Freed slaves were losing their freedom. Little by little they must have felt good about themselves that summer; now they were back to working like slaves. No, worse than slaves: They were being arrested and had to work out their fines like prisoners. This was wrong, wrong, wrong.

Why couldn't they have jobs that paid them? "Walls of Jericho!" He watched people climb onto the wagon.

With a nod, Gideon, Mr. Freedman, and five hired men disappeared in the direction of that wagon. Nelly and Pascal looked away. When they returned, Gideon wiped a smile from his face. Pascal wondered what they had done.

Soon people gathered for the Union League club meeting. Mr. McPherson, the Republican organizer, stepped up on a box in the street and introduced a captain of the Union army. Mr. McPherson was a busy man, thought Pascal, organizing on both sides of the Savannah.

The captain shouted, "We planned

parades for the Fourth of July, but we were fired on." He waved his arms. "Maybe the South hasn't heard. The war is over, and they lost!"

Everyone cheered loudly, but Pascal remembered when some colored people were even afraid to clap. Because he felt jittery, he took Nelly's hand and worked his way out of the crowd. He never liked being inside. Gideon and Mr. Freedman noticed him and followed. Soon they were sitting with their hired workers on the wooden sidewalk by the school.

The evening air cooled, and a breeze shook leaves on a nearby tree. The rustling leaves bothered Pascal. He saw Gideon begin to fidget, too. He bet Gideon was worried about the farm.

The captain's speech went on and on. They were punishing the wealthy plantation owners and the top officers of the Confederacy. Pascal wondered if that wouldn't make them angry. He felt hairs rise on the nape of his neck.

When Mr. McPherson climbed back on the box, he pointed to the lines of people still signing up for work contracts. "In Congress, Republicans will kill those Black Codes."

The cheers were softer.

"The South," he said, "wants to reverse Reconstruction with a Redemptorist policy. We won't let them, will we?"

"Oh, Lordy," a woman called, "the masters will get us back any way they can!" Pascal shuddered. That was true; new laws were taking them backward.

The first wagon pulled away loaded with sobbing colored people clinging to each other. When Pascal stood, he saw loose wheels on that wagon wobble. Now he knew what Gideon and the men had done. He wondered how long before the wagon would break down. Could the colored people escape?

"For all of you on Sherman Lands," Mr. McPherson yelled in a raspy voice, "good news! In Circular Thirteen you have the rights to your forty acres."

Gideon cheered, but Pascal shook Gideon's arm for an explanation. "At first," Gideon whispered, "General Sherman be giving out land to get rid of slaves following his troops. He just told folks to take land and begin farming. Now they done written it up as a right."

Gideon's smile made Pascal feel better. He looked up at the stars and whispered, "Thank you, Lord," but in the west he saw a glow.

He pointed and called, "Look, y'all. What's that over yonder?" The crowd stirred. Other people called out and stared. Suddenly the glow grew brighter and reflected off a wandering cloud.

"They're burning Jubilee Town," a woman screamed.

The shout went up. "Burning Jubilee Town!"

A man pushed Mr. McPherson off the box. He shouted, "Yes, that town and your lands are burning. That'll teach y'all a lesson. Go back to your masters!" He shook a fist. "Go back!"

Pascal remembered him from the road in South Carolina. He and an older man had been the night riders. What was he doing here in Georgia? It seemed the masters were closing in on them, trapping them.

Pascal, standing by the school, smelled smoke behind him. Yellow flames began to crackle and pop inside the storefront. The school shimmered in a heat puff, then burst into yellow tongues of fire. Pascal saw a white man walk away with a kerosene can.

He yelled, "No, no, no!" and shook his fist at that man. They were losing everything. Colored people were being carried back into slavery, and their school was going up in flames. Nelly began twisting her braids.

Gideon stood and shouted, "Stop it, stop!" Pascal caught Gideon's shirttail to keep him from chasing the man who had set the school on fire.

The hired men backed away. The women wrung their hands and moaned. Mr. Freedman caught Pascal, Nelly, and Gideon and dragged them away. Soon they were all running from the schoolhouse fire.

Gideon called, "What's happened to our forty acres? Oh, Lord!"

Chapter Sixteen

"Take it slow," Pascal shouted to Gideon as they ran. Pascal was tripping over his lame foot. "You'll drop before you reach there." Was their family farm safe? Had his plan worked?

Gideon sobbed into the night air. "I shouldn't have let no forty acres claim my heart," he called in gasps, "but that cotton fairly climbed out of the earth singing hallelujah! That land be giving glory to the Lord. Was gonna call it Green Gloryland."

"Green Gloryland!" Pascal began to cry. Would their crops still be growing? Nelly took his hand, but she was sniffing herself. Mr. Freedman had his arm around Gladness; they were bumping each other as they hurried. The hired men and women were comforting each other as they ran.

They took a bold shortcut through a white man's field. All were quiet until they reached a road again and could breathe easier.

Nelly said, "Ain't no red in the sky over yonder."

"Ain't no smoke rising, neither," said Mr. Freedman. "Remember how it smoked when we burned it?"

Pascal breathed deeply and clutched his walking stick. Had he outwitted the night riders for Gideon again? A breeze cooled the air, and Pascal felt cold from his sweat. This seemed to be the longest walk ever, but as they grew closer, the pain in his heart eased. No fire.

He saw a white cloth blowing on their hilltop. As the others spread out looking at the cotton and food crops, he ran to the hill. "Judith," he called. Yellow hair flowing, she stood on the hilltop, her full skirt billowing in the breeze.

"Pascal!" She ran downhill, and Matthew ran behind her.

"Did the night riders come? What happened?"

"We were playing under the Ghost Tree when the first riders with burning torches galloped up. They asked if these were Sherman Lands belonging to Negroes. Matthew shouted, 'No, to neighbors.' I'm so proud of him."

Judith was crying as she talked. "We were

afraid, so we came up here. Three other groups came by asking. They saw we were white, and rode on."

"Lord, thank you," Pascal called. His plan had saved the farm! He shouted, "They stopped the men. Green Gloryland is safe." He turned to Matthew. "How did you do it?"

Matthew raised his chin. "Miss Anderson made me shout, 'Good Morning.'" He turned to Judith. "I want to go back to school. Tomorrow, Judith, we go to school no matter what. Miss Anderson taught me to speak loud when I have to."

Nelly shook her head. "School?" she asked, arms folded.

When Gideon reached them, he was frowning. "We be going to Mister Deliverance's dairy farm. Got a worry about him. Looks like there be trouble; we see smoke over there."

"Walk Judith and Matthew home," Mr. Freedman told Pascal. Tears glistened in his eyes, but his jaw was set. Pascal lent Mr. Freedman his stick to defend himself.

"We should stay," Judith said. "We white people have to help. Ma says all those evil years . . ." She sobbed.

Pascal caught Judith's hand on one side; he caught Matthew's on his weak side. "Come on," he said. "Me and Nelly got something to tell you. Won't none of us be going to school tomorrow."

The next morning Pascal was awakened by a cowbell. He jumped up from lying under a tree, and sunlight high in the sky made him blink. His face grew warm from shame. He had overslept and Gideon was walking to the lake with a cow. Its brass bell tolled sadly.

"Where's Mister Deliverance?" Pascal called.

Gideon was streaked with ashes. He shook his head. "They strung him up on a tree; burned his grazing ground; shot all his cows. Old Bossy here ain't hurt bad."

Pascal put his hands over his ears. He didn't want to hear that! How dare they lynch happy, proud Mr. Alonzo Deliverance! Always so cheerful, he was their neighbor and friend.

And the danger had been so close. Suppose the City family had been on the farm — would they have strung up Gideon?

"Let me take the cow by the lake to graze," Pascal said tearfully. "We can share her milk with the Bibbs."

"Mister Freedman's bringing some wood of Mister Alonzo's over to build a smoke-house for the meat. The hired men be butchering the dead cows. We'll be having beef for a harvest celebration."

"Celebration?" Pascal asked as he took the cow's rope.

"We just buried Mister Deliverance without no proper funeral," Gideon said. "He be wanting a celebration to help him go to glory." Gideon wiped tears with the back of his hand and added: "He died a brave death. His wife said he told them, 'Y'all said I be too dumb to live free. Well, I made money, so I wasn't dumb. You can kill me, but y'all can't stop freedom.'"

"Where's his wife?" asked Pascal.

"She's taken their children into town. Gladness know a home where they be safe. Yes," Gideon said suddenly, shaking a fist, "they won't keep us from celebrating. We'll call it a Green Gloryland Jubilee."

In late July as he chopped cotton — loosening the dirt and digging weeds under — Pascal could smell cow meat smoking. His back was to the road, but sometimes he turned to see the folks.

The night riders had burned Jubilee Town to the ground. Families from the town had buried their dead, and now they were leaving. Moaning as they walked — mothers carrying infants, fathers carrying little ones, children hand in hand — a parade of

139

colored people passed on the road, lugging all they owned. They were looking for a life somewhere else.

But how far could they go before they would be arrested for what the white people called *vagrancy?* Pascal wondered. They would be given over to white people to work without pay for a year. It seemed the masters were winning after all. Could the City family escape?

The smell of beef strips smoking was sweet but sad.

Mr. Freedman kept only enough meat for the City and Bibb families for the winter. All day he stood by the road. "Food — strips of beef and fresh vegetables, brother. Meat for the children, sister," he called to people marching past.

Pascal made sure Mr. Freedman asked, "Do any of y'all know any men be sons of Jerusalem City from South Carolina?" Day after day people shook their heads.

But they called, "Thank you, brother," and took the food: beef, turnips, beans, potatoes, squash.

Brother? Sister? Yes, thought Pascal, in bad times and good, we all be family. He was looking for three brothers, but maybe he belonged to a bigger family? Pascal scratched a mosquito bite.

A group passed, singing in harmony, "'Nobody knows the trouble I seen, nobody knows but Jesus.'"

One day Mr. Freedman walked back to Pascal. "No more food to pass out," he said. "All gone excepting what be for us. The folks don't get too far." He sighed. "I'll get my hoe. The Bibbs need help." Pascal nodded.

Soon it was time to eat supper under the trees. To call, Pascal whistled like a red-winged blackbird. They ate and rested under the cool willows by the lake. There were no whippings, no insults, no thirst, no hunger as when they worked in slavery. Gideon was a good boss man, and Mr. Freedman helped him.

Soon, it was August. Pascal felt a heartache. I feel guilty, he decided, guilty that we still have Green Gloryland. And fearful. How long could they outwit the white people?

Heat waves shimmered in the glaring sunshine of late summer, and even the bumblebees buzzed complaints. Cotton was bursting open for picking; the harvest had begun. One day in August Gideon ran to Pascal. "Drop your bag and come see!"

"One more row to pick," Pascal said,

wiping his forehead. He had just gotten up from sleeping in the row. He didn't really want to keep on, but he wanted Gideon to think he did. Gideon was the fastest and best worker in the cotton fields. Pascal was by far the slowest and worst picker, but he told himself his role was to keep the farm safe.

"I be boss on Green Gloryland, and I say stop!"

Pascal dropped the long sack he used to hold his cotton. "Yes, sir, boss man." He grinned in relief.

A running Gideon dragged Pascal behind him. "Did you find something?" Pascal asked, limping and tripping.

"Wait and see," Gideon said as they crossed the field. They slid under the roots of the Ghost Tree where Gladness sat sewing. "Glory, glory," she said, laughing.

"What it be?" Pascal asked. "Sit down," said Gideon. "I ain't had time to get back to this hole, but now I think I got me something." He dug loose dirt from a side of the earth cavern. Pascal heard a click and leaned forward.

"Well, lookee here," Gideon said, laughing. He pulled out a rusted metal box that had been buried in the hole, pulled it out as if he hadn't seen it before. And suddenly

Pascal knew he had dug it out earlier and planted it again so Pascal could watch. When Pascal opened the top, he saw shiny yellow coins.

"Gold," he whispered.

"Plenty coins for all of us and for the Bibbs," said Gideon. "We got us some money for the future of Green Gloryland."

"It's a treasure box," Pascal said, touching the gold.

"You be right."

Gladness held up what she was stitching in her lap. "You'll keep this and wear it if we go into town." She had fit slots for gold coins inside Gideon's Union cap, and with the gold in place the cap fit Pascal.

Gideon tossed a handful of gold coins in the air. They clinked cheerfully. "Let me hand these out right fast," he said, "before I get greedy. I don't wanna be slave to no gold, like the white man. Mama wouldn't like me to be selfish. Poor Mama."

Pascal nodded. Mama was never selfish or greedy; never let "things" rule her life; she always thought about helping folks. She died asking for more food for others. Why couldn't she have kept silent like everyone else? Why, Mama?

Chapter Seventeen

True to his promise, Gideon gave gold coins to all his workers, to the Bibbs, and to his family. The hired workers were astonished. "Lordy," a woman said, "ain't enough our boss man give us food and a house to sleep in. Now he giving out gold!"

With a swagger, Gideon answered, "You be getting more pay at cotton settlement time. This be your early pay."

Pascal smiled. He loved his brother's generosity. Gideon had offered jobs to many freed slaves on the road, and because of their work the family farm was beautiful. Pascal suspected that it made his brother feel like a "big man" to be generous.

"Your land yielded a crop of gold," said Mrs. Bibb when she received her family's share. "Somebody must have buried it there for safekeeping. But, if they ain't returned for it, and since you got title to the land, I reckon it's yours. Thank you, Gideon. Now maybe our children will never never never be hungry again."

Pascal and Nelly knew where their gold was hidden in the house. Any time they wanted, they could take out the coins and play with them. Nelly shined fingerprints off her coins. Pascal liked to hear the *clink clink* of the gold. Now he was a landowner with gold. But he wondered: How much difference did it really make?

Since there was no school to attend, Pascal and Nelly picked cotton all day. In the hot August evenings the whole City family, owners, and hired people sang and ginned cotton — picking out seeds by hand. Gideon had pounds of cotton — ginned and ready for baling — in their farmhouse, and more cotton opened each day for picking.

Mr. Freedman and workers had been digging a well. By the end of August they reached a muddy dampness that promised good well water.

One September evening the Bibb children played hide-and-go-seek under the Ghost Tree with Pascal and Nelly. A stumbling Pascal kept looking over his shoulder, watching the road. He couldn't find Gladness and Gideon anywhere. All day they had been whispering together and then they had disappeared.

"Oh," Nelly called, "it be mystery-of-the-world time. Hurry, hurry!" Judith and Matthew ran over to her. Glancing at the road one more time, Pascal limped toward them.

"When the stars come out," said Nelly, "you gotta raise your hands so the world goes on."

"And if you don't?" Judith asked, dancing from foot to foot.

Nelly shook her head solemnly. "T'would be too terrible to tell," she said. "Lucky for us so far, somewhere, somehow, a child raises hands to the sky in mystery-of-the-world time."

"Oh," said Matthew, "you think children make the world go 'round? Would Pa approve? This ain't about the evil one, is it?" He backed into a row of cotton.

"'Course not. You can say anything you want. But you say it in your heart."

Matthew smiled. "I'll say, 'Praise the Lord'!"

"Me, too," said Judith. As a lavender blanket spread over the sky, they all raised their arms.

With relief Pascal pointed. "Here come Gideon and Gladness at last."

Nelly said, "I think I know what they'll say."

"Really?" asked Judith as they ran toward Gladness.

"Wait and see," sang Nelly, skipping on barefoot toes.

Gideon whistled for everyone to gather around. "Bad news first," he told everyone. "In town they calling a big meeting Friday night to tell about Sherman Lands. Don't know what it say, but there be a new Circular Fifteen for September."

He shook his head, and Mr. Freedman moaned.

Gideon pointed to Pascal and the other children. "And good news. School be open again. Miss Anderson and Miss Harris be using new supplies to teach outdoors excepting on rainy days. Nobody in town had spunk enough to rent them a place for school — not even for white people's children." He shook his head. "Folks be running scared."

School sounded wonderful to Pascal. Now that things were so uncertain, he needed that school learning more than ever.

Then Gideon looked at Gladness and began stuttering. "Since we don't have no colored church nor minister in town, the Freedmen's Bureau man be our official.

147

He's leaving town tomorrow, but before he does, he be coming to visit."

He cleared his throat and gazed at Gladness, who swirled her full skirt. "He be coming to marry me and Gladness."

Nelly cheered and ran around them, clapping. Pascal stared at Nelly. How come she knew about it and he didn't? He opened his mouth and couldn't shut it. Wasn't Gideon too young? What would Mama say?

On the other hand, since Gladness had joined them, Gideon seemed happier. Maybe Gladness was good for Gideon?

Nelly ran to hug Pascal. He tried to smile, but his face felt stiff, as if it might break into pieces. Would he lose his brother? His family? He still wasn't sure he liked the idea of Gideon marrying.

Emmanuel called, "Celebration time! Jubilee night! Hurry, Judith, Matthew, tell your folks. Tell the neighbors. Tomorrow night we am celebrating a wedding!"

The next night there was a timid thin moon and it smiled crookedly on them. Neighbors colored and white had come from farms and from town. Fires roared in pits surrounded by stones.

Gladness wore her best skirt and a dozen red, yellow, green, and blue ribbons in her hair. Gideon wore a clean shirt and his army boots.

By the light of the fires, Gideon promised his vows to Gladness, and Gladness promised her vows to Gideon. A smiling Mr. Freedman rubbed his hands. He held a broom under one arm. After Gideon and Gladness had said the words for the official, they married the way colored people did on the plantations.

"Hurry and get the broom," Emmanuel called, but Mr. Freedman had it.

Hired workers shouted, "Jump the broom, jump the broom!" They were clapping to encourage the bride and groom.

Pascal and Nelly each held an end of the broom. Laughing, Gideon and Gladness held hands and looked at each other. Colored people called, "Jump the broom!"

Finally Gideon and Gladness ran up to the broom and jumped over. That meant they were ready to start keeping a home together.

"That be the broom I made, you know," Nelly whispered to Pascal as she stood it against a rock. He nodded. He had never thought it would be used for his brother's wedding. He stared at the wedding group.

The portly Freedmen's Bureau man looked nervous as usual. This time he kept glancing over his shoulder at the road. Pascal could understand his nervousness. With Black Codes, hangings, fires, shootings, threats — this man had been brave to remain in River Stop this long. Pascal had seen him shot at once. How often since that day in April had the man suffered threats?

After everyone congratulated the newlyweds, Mr. Bibb stood with a wrapped lard bucket in his arms. "Mr. and Mrs. City," he said, "these are yours for all Green Gloryland people to enjoy."

Gideon uncovered two sturdy green plants about two hands high and separated in the bucket. As Gideon held it, Gladness fingered the leaves. "Glory be to heaven, y'all," she said. "Thank you. These here be apple trees."

"Apple trees?" With a smile, Gideon glanced around. He seemed to be looking for a place to plant them.

"We brought the seedlings all the way from Tennessee," said Mrs. Bibb, smiling. "We just planted our trees last week."

Next a hired man from River Stop gave Gladness a rooster and three hens. "You can have eggs all winter and hatch chicks for the springtime," he said.

"We got wood for a chicken coop," said Mr. Freedman, rubbing his hands.

"Tomorrow I'll get started to build one."

Pascal turned to Nelly and Judith. "Do y'all know why chickens sleep on one leg?"

"No, why?" asked Nelly.

"Cause if they pulled up that leg, they'd fall."

The girls giggled.

People congratulated Gladness and Gideon as they stood on the hillside. Neighbors sat on the ground, and Nelly started dancing around the cooking fire. Pascal joined her skipping and stepping and swaying around and around. He felt better about Gideon being married than he had the day before. Maybe Gladness would help keep Gideon from doing foolish things. Maybe their marriage was all right.

"Sing a song 'bout an apple tree,
Happy now we all be free,
Gonna eat apples offen our tree,
Sing a song 'bout an apple tree,"

sang Nelly.

Gideon passed with a shovel and bucket.

"Can't you wait to plant them tomorrow?" Gladness called. Gideon shook his head no. He was fairly running.

Judith and Matthew followed Pascal, skipping and swaying and dancing around the fires, but they kept glancing at their pa. Naomi sucked her thumb and skipped in place by her mother.

Mr. Bibb said, "Most Baptists don't believe in dancing. But I reckon if King David could dance before the Ark, it's all right to dance. So long as it's praising the Lord." Mr. Bibb raised his fiddle and caught the rhythm of the music.

Emmanuel served beef boiled with cabbage, and turnips and tomatoes. They ate mixed greens — turnip tops, spinach, and lettuce, seasoned with onions and smoked beef. The children drank boiled milk, the grown-ups drank boiled coffee. Kettles of food and pots of coffee filled the air with good smells mingled with laughter.

A smiling Emmanuel told Pascal, "This be the most perfect jubilee I ever did see. The way it should be. Colored and white, we're all just neighbors."

Pascal added wood, and the yellow fires danced higher as the night grew darker. He visited colored people he had not seen before and asked, "We looking for three brothers sold from my mama. Her name be Jerusalem City, and we from South Carolina."

"Sorry," one man said.

"Hope you find your brothers," said another.

Someone else promised, "I'll pass word for you." Pascal turned away sadly. At least he had Gideon.

After he planted his trees, Gideon called for silence. He said, "Mister Alonzo Deliverance celebrates with us from the heavenly Gloryland — him and thousands like him. Lord, remember them, and give us your strength." He looked down. Everyone stood silently among crackling fires and insect calls.

Pascal felt a choking sadness. He glanced at the road and stood straight. Danger.

"Amen!" Gideon called, and waved at Mr. Bibb to begin fiddling again. Pascal ran over and whispered in his ear. Suddenly, his fiddle died. With a glance toward the road, Mr. Bibb raised the fiddle again and began the slow Virginia reel. Pascal waved to Judith.

Judith beckoned to Matthew, curtsied, then held her skirt to the side to dance. Matthew glanced toward the road, then danced. Several other white people took hands to dance, stiffly and stately — bowing, crossing over, promenading.

Pascal ran down the hill and pushed his tall brother to sit down. White people danced on the hilltop, putting themselves by the light of the fires, while Pascal waved for colored people to draw back into shadows.

Everyone caught the idea in a short time.

"Look," Pascal whispered to Gideon and Nelly, and pointed.

A carriage rolled slowly down the road. Balancing to keep from falling, the man beside the driver stood and watched the dance on the hillcrest. Mr. Bibb began calling a square dance next. When the carriage reached the end of Green Gloryland, the driver turned the carriage around and the horses clip-clopped slowly by Gideon's farm again. Then they were gone.

Judith laughed and ran to Pascal. "We fooled them again," she called. Her breath smelled of turnip greens and onions.

The barrel-shaped Freedmen's Bureau man silently handed Gideon and Gladness their wedding papers. Wiping his mouth, he hustled down the hill. As he rode off, he gave a quick wave. Gideon and Gladness stood side by side, watching him leave.

When the wedding guests left for home, Gideon stood by the road. Carrying his walking stick, Pascal joined him. After a while, his eyes were closing. "Come on, Gideon," he said, "we got to sleep. Gladness be waiting for you back at the house."

Gideon moaned. "I feel it be only a matter of time."

"Time till what?"

"Time till I lose my farm. Just a few of us colored that ain't been shot at, or burned out, or scared away. It be just a matter of time."

"No, no, Gideon," said Pascal. "Things gonna change soon. Nelly and me be helping you keep the farm safe. Besides, if we lost it, what would we do?"

Gideon glared at him and started toward the house. Pascal limped behind him.

He thought back from April, through May, June, July, August, and now into September. He remembered escaping in the night from their master; the man who shot at Mr. Freedman; the woman who said President Lincoln deserved to die for freeing people's property; the night riders saying they shot the uppity colored people and captured the submissive ones; the Black Codes for vagrancy laws; the work contracts they signed; the lynching of Mr. Deliverance; the burning of colored people's fields; the burning of Jubilee Town; the burning of the schoolhouse. What kind of freedom was this?

Why couldn't white people just let them live?

Chapter Eighteen

The next September morning was born singing. Rosy tints of sunrise rippled on clouds, and the tiny pink cloud puffs scudded about the sky.

Early in the day, from his row in the cotton field, Pascal saw Gideon on the hillcrest. Something about his rigid posture made Pascal drop his hoe and limp slowly toward the house. Something was wrong; he felt it in his bones. Was there something he could do to help?

Mr. Freedman and Emmanuel, who had been digging the well, stood leaning on shovels. Hired men and women followed their rows of cotton back to the house. As Pascal passed, he saw Gladness catch Nelly's arm and pull her along.

A white man passed Pascal in the field. Why did he look familiar? The bushy eyebrows. Of course, he had seemed taller on a horse, but this was the other night rider from South Carolina. He walked ahead of a young man who could have been his son. The older man gestured wildly, looking from side to side. The young man followed, staring straight ahead. Neither noticed Pascal.

"Not a boll weevil to be seen. Cleanest crop I ever saw," said the father. "A lake for watering, a creek for wading water. We'll make a killing in cotton off this land!"

Pascal frowned. This was their land; what did that white man mean? When he reached Gideon's side on the hill, he saw Mr. McPherson walking toward the bottom of the hillcrest. Mr. McPherson's white handkerchief fluttered about his face.

"Mister City," he called, "the Southern farmers have caught the ear of President Johnson, it seems. They're suffering from crops poorly planted and no workers for picking."

Lowering his voice, he said, "They lived for two hundred years on slave labor, and now they're suffering. They want former slaves to return to their plantation fields."

With a sigh, he went on. "Circular Fifteen says Sherman Lands are only available to white people. All former slaves must give up their lands." He wiped his face.

Walls of Jericho! Pascal staggered back and sank to the ground. His weak arm began to twitch, and he held it. The white man had won. The colored people hadn't escaped after all. Was there something they could do?

Could they hide and sneak out and kill the white people in the night? No, other colored people would suffer. White people would have an excuse to take revenge on the coloreds.

The City family stood like pine trees in a forest. Still. Silent. A breeze became playful and blew Emmanuel's red bandanna and Gladness's hair ribbons. Her skirt flapped in the breeze.

Why wasn't Gideon fighting? They were all so quiet, Pascal thought. Accepting what white people did. And yet, he realized, they couldn't fight back.

The man returned from touring the cotton field. "Mister McPherson," he said, "I'll take this here farm." His words were slow and Southern. He pointed uphill to Gideon and swept his arm to three hired men and Emmanuel. "I'll use these Negroes at our other plantation," he said. "Get your man to write up their work contracts."

How dare this man say things like that, thought Pascal.

The man pointed to Mr. Freedman. "I may keep him here," he said, his voice rumbling. "Unless the old man's not worth it. We don't have to care for the old people anymore." He laughed and slapped his son's shoulder.

Pascal trembled in fury. Couldn't this man understand how they felt? It seemed colored people were less than cattle to this man.

The man looked at Nelly and Gladness. "The women" — he paused and rubbed his cheek — "I can use one for my wife's personal maid, and the other in my daughter's kitchen in Carolina. Those other women can go."

Pascal felt like screaming. How dare he speak of Nelly and Gladness like that! Then the man noticed Pascal sitting by himself.

He walked up the hillcrest and nudged Pascal with his shoe. "A withered hand and leg," he said, wrinkling his nose as if smelling something stinky. He turned to Mr. McPherson and called, "You said you knew these people. Can the boy talk?"

A red-faced Mr. McPherson turned and walked away without answering. His shoulders seemed caught in a painful clamp.

The man kicked Pascal gently and shouted at him, "Tell me. What's your name, boy?"

159

Pascal held his twitching arm closer to his heart, and his head high in defiance. He didn't have to answer this white man. How dare this man take their farm!

In keeping silent, not doing what the man asked, he felt triumphant. It was the first time in his whole life that he hadn't obeyed a white man. The defiance, the triumph, was this what Mama felt? Was this what Gideon felt?

Something surged inside him, some new feeling. Freedom? Yes! He felt strong and black and free. He was somebody, and had done what was good: farming, caring for folks. This man was wrong, wrong, wrong

"That boy's deaf and crippled," said the man. "We'll get rid of him!"

For the first time, being called crippled didn't hurt Pascal's feelings. His weak arm and leg didn't make him any less of a person. HE WAS SOMEBODY, AND AL-WAYS HAD BEEN. Was that what Mama had known? She had asked for food for dying slaves. Maybe Mama had known freedom after all! Master may have owned her work, but her spirit was free!

Maybe nobody gave freedom, and nobody could take it away like they could take away a family farm. Maybe freedom was something you claimed for yourself.

Mr. McPherson called to Gideon. "Sorry, but it's his farm now, Mister City. And don't forget, vote Republican!" He waved. At the road he mounted a horse and rode away.

The man and his son had arrived in the same carriage that had passed the night before. With a hesitant glance at Gideon and the other men, they strode across the farm and climbed in their carriage as the breeze noisily flapped Gladness's skirt.

When the father and son were out of sight, Pascal yelled and leaped up. Why wasn't someone doing something? Gideon looked as limp as wet underwear. Pascal ran downhill to the dugout well and furiously pushed dirt back in. Those white men would not have the well they had spent weeks digging. That was something he could do!

Over his shoulder Pascal saw Nelly and Gladness hugging each other and weeping.

Mr. Freedman straightened his back. Glancing at Pascal, he ran for his tools and began hammering loose the corner doors of the house.

Emmanuel followed Pascal's lead, too. He shoveled dirt back in the well with a vengeance. When dirt flew in his eye, Pascal ran up the hill to their house. Head down, he banged a fist against their porch post.

Gideon caught his hand. Pascal saw that

161

his knuckles were bleeding, but he hadn't felt the pain. Gideon gently squeezed Pascal's wrist and hugged his little brother. Sobbing, Pascal clung to his brother's side. He remembered when Gideon first heard that Mama was dead, and they had hugged like this. He felt Gideon crying silently. This had been their family farm, their life — and now white people said they couldn't keep it. For moments he thought the pain would kill him. How could he go on? What could he do?

"Hurry," he heard Mr. Freedman call. "We'll move the farmhouse. I'm thinking the Bibbs will need a house this winter, and those white men ain't getting it."

"Won't the men recognize it?" Gladness asked.

"Not when I finish," said her grandfather. He turned to the hired men and women both. "Hurry."

Pascal raised his head. Something else he could do. He ran down the hill and grabbed a hammer.

Gideon raced to his shovel. Over his shoulder Pascal saw his brother dig up his apple trees and put them back in the lard bucket. After Gideon finished, he joined everyone taking down the farmhouse. They ripped it apart and broke it into sections to carry.

As wall after wall was pulled down, lifted, and carried around the lake, Pascal covered the ginned cotton to keep it from blowing. What had taken seven days to move now took seven hours. Everyone worked furiously without orders, and without food. Pascal thought maybe anger gave them all strength. At the Bibbs's farm he and Nelly sweated as they helped fill a trench with the base stones. His fingers were bleeding, and his weak side trembled.

Mrs. Bibb sat crying with little Naomi at her side. "There's no justice! You been so very very very kind. Buried our dead sons. Fed us when we were sick and starving for want of food. Real neighbors. I just can't understand it."

Sitting shoulder to shoulder, Judith and Matthew sobbed.

When the porch posts were in place, Mr. Freedman nailed wood across them. "Nobody can recognize the house now, and I reckon Alonzo's cow and the wedding chickens can sleep here in winter," he told Mr. Bibb. "Alonzo Deliverance will bless you.

"Now where's that can of whitewash?" he called. "Gideon, you're tall with arms long enough. You paint the top of the house wall, and Pascal can cover the bottom."

"We don't have paintbrushes," said Pascal. It was evening, and he covered his eyes from the setting sun.

Mr. Freedman handed him a piece of shirt rag. "Use this. Just one wiping." He sighed. "I was planning to paint the inside to make it bright and cheerful for winter. But . . ."

"The paint will fool them white men," Matthew said. He dipped a rag and began wiping the logs.

Pascal stared at Matthew. Didn't he realize he was white, too? Those other white men didn't even realize that colored folks were human. But it wasn't skin color; other white people — President Lincoln, Master's mother, Mr. McPherson — they knew what was right.

Pascal felt a strange power. He held his breath and fisted his hands. Inside him surged a wave of dignity. He was somebody even without land! He was free, and nothing — lame leg, weak arm, family farm taken away, torn pants — nothing else mattered. Inside him blossomed the freedom that had been growing. It seemed to burst his chest. He promised himself to never let it go.

Mama had known freedom. She was free to tell the truth; now he understood. And maybe they'd find land for a family farm somewhere else? He had to hope.

Matthew was painting the bottom of the house. Pascal covered the lower middle; Gideon wiped whitewash up to the roof. They covered two and a half sides facing the road before the whitewash ran out.

"Good job," said Mr. Freedman. He showed Mr. Bibb how the corner doors worked. "To get out in case of fire or trouble."

Last of all they dragged sacks of ginned cotton from Green Gloryland. Now that the Bibb family could move into the farmhouse, their wagon had been emptied. Pascal helped fill the Bibbs's wagon with ginned cotton. Gideon covered the cotton with their canvas tent top.

After that they sat around eating and crying together by the lake as the thin moon rose. Sitting between Nelly and Judith, Pascal thought about their forty acres, their family farm. He had helped Gideon ask for it, and he had outwitted some of the night riders. For months he had worked the farm the best he could, and he felt proud of that.

For many years colored people in America had farmed other people's land, and their work had been stolen, Pascal thought. Now they were free, and their farm had been stolen.

He wondered if Gideon thought of burning the rest of the cotton, the part that was still in the field. But, no. They had worked too hard to tend that cotton field, that Green Gloryland. He knew Gideon loved that cotton, and in spite of being a slow, maybe even lazy worker, Pascal was proud of it, too.

After supper Emmanuel stood. Hired men and women stood with him. He blew his nose, and wiped tears with the back of his hand. Nelly began twisting her braids.

Chapter Nineteen

Pascal sat cross-legged, looking at the stars. He wondered if Nelly had raised her arms. "It be mystery-of-the-world time," he whispered.

"Some other child got to do it tonight," she said. "My heart be fairly broken. I hope them boll weevils come and eat up all that cotton. I hope them white men don't get none of our crop." Her tears rolled like rain.

"We knew it be coming."

Pascal felt numb. All day he had worked moving and painting the farmhouse and he was bone-tired. He supposed he had always known deep inside that they would never keep Green Gloryland.

Emmanuel cleared his throat. "There be a restaurant in town need a good cook," he said, "but I reckon I'll come around to help y'all pick your cotton crop." He shook hands with Mr. Bibb. "Any of us hired men. We be just in River Stop."

Gideon stood, and Emmanuel hugged him. The other hired men and women followed Emmanuel, shaking hands with Mr. Bibb, then embracing Gideon. Some looked as if they wanted to speak, but they were too choked up. Several held up pieces of gold, as if thanking Gideon again.

As they trudged away, Pascal called, "Keep your work contracts. Maybe they won't catch you."

Next, Mr. Freedman cleared his throat. "There be plenty work for a carpenter in River Stop. I reckon I'll spend the night where Gladness used to work. They be good people what know about freedom. And when you find another land to farm, Gladness be knowing where to find me."

Gladness nodded and hugged him. Passing Gideon his work contract, Mr. Freedman said, "Seeing as though you can't keep the farm, I reckon you'll need this." He limped away, head high.

Pascal looked after them, and his heart ached. The farm family was breaking up. At least they got to keep Gladness. His heart ached for all the workers; they were all somebody. He realized that now. People didn't need to own land to be somebody.

Mrs. Bibb told Gideon, Gladness, Pascal, and Nelly, "I would be very very very happy if you would spend the night."

"No thanks, ma'am," Gideon said. He slapped his heavy Union cap on Pascal and picked up his apple trees. "We be going now, too." Gladness walked by his side, a clothes bundle over her shoulder. Carrying her shawl sack, Nelly followed them. Pascal grasped his walking stick, hung his potato sack of belongings on it, and followed them.

He waved to Judith and Matthew. "See you in school tomorrow."

They spent the night in the pine-woods cave — Pascal and Nelly on either side of the entrance, Gideon and Gladness cuddled together inside. Stick in hand, Pascal kept an uneasy watch. Were they safe anywhere?

The next morning Gideon said, "You and Nelly go to school. I be scouting for the road to the Sea Islands. There be farms there, I hear, and once I find the road, we be on our way."

When Gideon left, Nelly sat on the ground outside the cave and said, "I be glad we going to another farm."

"Do you mind going? We be hiding like before," Pascal said as he leaned against the rocky ledge.

"So long as we be family, and them Sea Islands have them same stars and moon and sun. . . ." She choked up.

Pascal said, "You know what? I been thinking a lot about freedom." He touched his chest. "Freedom be here, like you said. Can't nobody take it away."

And he thought: Thank you, Mama.

Looking uphill, Pascal pointed. "School be only a little ways from here." Glancing at his hands, he noticed dirt deep under his nails. He brushed his hair, and Nelly combed her braids, but he was worried. He could wash up at the river, but it was way far down the hillside. With such dirty hands and face, he might not be allowed to sit with the others.

He and Nelly reached the wooded roadside where the teachers promised to hold school. Judith and Matthew weren't there. In fact, for the first time there were no white children. Were they lost? Were they scared? Thirty or more colored students skipped around and waited. Seven adults, four men and three women, stood by the road with arms folded. None of the men looked like possible family.

In the distance he saw Miss Anderson and Miss Harris trudging down the road, each holding a side of a wooden box of school supplies. Miss Anderson's long brown hair flopped loose of her comb, and she simply

170

tucked it back with one hand.

"Good morning, students," she said.

"Good morning, Miss Anderson. Good morning, Miss Harris."

"Any new students?" asked Miss Harris. She counted. "Six? Good! Come over here for letters and object counting."

Nelly was told to sound out words in a story. Pascal sat under a tree with advanced students, and Miss Anderson handed him a book.

"This is reading for comprehension, Pascal. I'll question you in a few minutes." Her pale gray eyes seemed more gentle.

"Miss Anderson," he said, "they took our family farm, so me and Nelly don't have to leave early today."

She tilted her head and sighed. "Miss Harris," she said, "they took their farm, too."

Miss Harris shook her head sadly.

When Pascal reached for the book, he thought Miss Anderson would comment on his dirty fingernails. But he opened his mouth and stared. Miss Anderson's hands were smeared with dirt as well.

As she leaned over him, a wisp of long brown hair tickled his ear. She let it hang loose. And her long black skirt was dusty. When some children whispered, Miss

Anderson looked over at them. "It's all right to talk in order to help each other."

Mouth open, a boy near Pascal said, "Miss Anderson, last time when I talked, you hit my hand with your ruler."

"I'm sorry, Andrew James. I don't have time anymore for hitting people. I only have time for teaching, and precious little of that." She stared up into the long-needle pine beside her and sighed. "Besides, you boys and girls have been whipped enough in your lives."

Pascal saw her glance at raised scars on the boy's neck. She shuddered. Miss Anderson had learned, too, he thought.

Later he reported on his reading, a story of Rebecca and Isaac. After his report, Miss Anderson shook his hand. "Well done! Here's a newspaper to keep. You must read every day to stay a good reader, Pascal." He stared at the hand she had shaken.

Next she gave him number stories involving fractions. She explained how they were done. "Here's a slate for working them. Call me if you have any trouble." Walking away, she knelt in pine needles by Nelly.

Pascal stared at the slate and chalk. He'd never used a slate before. He loved the fact that it was so smooth and the rag erased it completely. He could write up to six problems at a time, and if he jiggled the slate, the numbers didn't slide away as they did in the dirt box.

At noon Nelly looked at him and left her reading group. It was time to go.

"Thank you, Miss Anderson," he called. "I don't know about tomorrow."

She hugged him to her side. "Try your best, Pascal."

Miss Harris waved from a circle of children listening as she read a story.

Taking Nelly's hand, Pascal limped away, smiling. Things can turn around, he thought. Times and people do change. After all, since April he had been freed, he had owned a family farm, and Miss Anderson had hugged him!

Chapter Twenty

As he limped away from the outdoor school, Pascal told Nelly, "There's gonna be some howling at the meeting Friday when they tell all those colored folks they gotta leave their farms."

She sighed. "Seems like everything now is a 'taking away.' They 'take away' walking free on the roads. They 'take away' farming free on our farms."

"But," Pascal said, "we can BE free. We can do what be good and right." He touched his chest and thought about Mama.

After supper with Gideon and Gladness at the cave, Pascal asked Gideon, "Do you got that treasure box?" He crouched in the cave opening. It was after sunset by then, and the hillside felt the comfort of lavender darkness covering it like a blanket.

Gideon pulled the rusty iron box from his sack. "I been thinking," he began.

"Me, too," Pascal said.

Gideon took out his title to the Sherman Lands farm. Pascal pointed. "That should be back in that hole."

"Why? No, no," Gladness said. "We away from all that now. Don't go back. That man might be there. Might be trouble."

Gideon kept his eyes on Pascal. "The high grass gonna hide us getting to the tree. . . ."

"And the hole be deep under the roots," said Pascal. He turned to Gladness. "We be careful. We men have something to do."

"We family have something to do," said Nelly. She knelt and began to search in her shawl sack.

"Why would you put something back for the white masters to find?" asked Gladness, shaking her head.

"No white man's gonna crawl under that tree," Gideon said. "But, some colored worker might dig down there at night. If he be curious. Like me."

"Yes," said Pascal. He searched in his bag for his work contract in case someone caught them, and for something else. Then he crawled to the opening and stood up.

"Watch things for us," Gideon told Gladness, and he touched her shoulder. "Don't worry. We be safe."

Keeping to shadows along the road, and

hiding in the bushes when a carriage passed, they finally reached Green Gloryland. It looked so peaceful with neat rows of cotton, some showing white fluff in the darkness. The willow trees lining the creek whispered in the breeze. Pascal's heart ached over their lost family farm. They crept to the Ghost Tree and slid into the root hole.

Pascal heard his heart drumming in his ears. He held the rusty box while his brother dug the loose wall.

"That be deep enough," said Gideon, resting his army shovel.

"A treasure box for someone else to find," said Nelly.

After Gideon folded his useless title and placed it in the bottom of the box, Nelly dropped in a gold coin. Pascal was surprised. He dropped a gold coin in, too. So, he and Nelly had been thinking alike. Gideon dropped in three gold coins that clinked against theirs. Nelly giggled.

After replacing the box, Gideon packed the hole firm. Pascal pressed the loose dirt with his hand, and Nelly added some stones over the dirt.

"I talked to some folks," said Gideon the next morning. "They say there be a road going east that meets a stream through the woods to the ocean. Then we ask about Georgia's Sea Islands." Sipping water, they ate smoked beef strips and stale biscuits for breakfast.

Pointing to his apple trees, Gideon's face quivered. "We gonna plant them apple trees on a new farm. This time we gonna buy us land." He shook his fist and looked to the heavens. "Ain't nobody taking away our next farm!"

"I know," said Gladness, hugging her husband.

Glancing at the apple trees, Pascal thought about the plantation whipping tree. He thought about the Ghost Tree, a tree of reward. These little apple trees were for the future; trees to keep them healthy with apples red and round, sweet and crunchy. Tender little trees of life!

After they ate breakfast, Gideon asked, "Y'all ready to go?"

"We could rest a couple of days, I reckon," said Pascal. He sniffed the air. It had rained earlier in the morning, and the woods were cool and fragrant.

"Rest? We ain't done nothing but rest." Gideon tossed his shovel and knapsack on his back. "Well? Y'all ready? Eighty miles to walk. I can't hardly wait to buy a new farm."

"I can't hardly wait to go to a new school

to learn about bookkeeping," Pascal said.

"I can't hardly wait for a new school to teach me store clerking," said Nelly.

Gladness picked up the apple trees, and Gideon led them uphill. "We'll take to the woods as soon as there's people on the road. Can't risk no planters catching us." He turned and smiled at them over his shoulder.

Pascal smiled back.

By the road, crushed grass clean from the night rain smelled good to Pascal. The rising sun made a double rainbow in the sky: violet, blue, green, yellow, orange, red — glowing in joyful loveliness. The rainbow seemed like a good sign, and Pascal loved the word *joy*.

Mama had said that peace was joy resting, and joy was peace dancing. Mama knew all about peace and joy, and freedom, too.

What a beautiful September morning, Pascal thought as they headed east into the sunrise. Nelly pointed to long shadows behind them. "See if you can run away from your shadow," she called. They ran ahead of Gideon and Gladness.

"Walls of Jericho! " Pascal called as he ran limping along. "Not only be I somebody, with a family all my own, but I feel as free as an eagle in the sky!"

Author's Note

In *Forty Acres and Maybe a Mule*, Pascal, Gideon, and Nelly march onto the pages to tell the human story of April through September 1865 in the complicated era of Reconstruction. After months of research, I have written a story as true as I could, not only in historical facts, but also in human feelings.

Reconstruction tried to answer questions: What to do with four million African Americans freed from slavery? What to do with the Confederate States that had fought against the Union?

President Abraham Lincoln made the first Reconstruction plan at the time of the Emancipation Proclamation in 1863; it was followed by plans in 1864 and 1866; by the Thirteenth and Fourteenth Amendments; and by the Reconstruction Acts of 1867, which sent Union troops into the South to help insure freedom for the slaves.

As soon as the War Between the States ended, Republicans began holding mass meetings and parades. They registered black voters and established Union League clubs in the South where blacks gathered to discuss national politics.

In January of 1865, to rid himself of thousands of "contraband" — runaway slaves who had followed his army through the South — General William Tecumseh Sherman issued Field Order 15, which gave out land. In July, Circular 13, issued by the Bureau of Refugees, Freedmen, and Abandoned Lands (the Freedmen's Bureau), approved the plan to give forty acres to any former slave family. It said the federal government might also provide a mule, but no mules were given out.

Under General Oliver O. Howard, 40,000 African Americans began farming on forty acres in that spring of 1865. The Freedmen's Bureau also set up schools, hospitals, asylums, and orphanages for the poor, both black and white.

What Circular 13 officially gave in July, Circular 15 in September of that year officially took back from former slaves. Of 40,000 freed people farming land, all but 1,565 lost their land. Those who kept land lived mostly on the Sea Islands off the coasts of Georgia and the Carolinas.

In spite of this tragedy, Reconstruction was a glorious period for freed African Americans. For a time they could vote, and they were elected to office. Forty-one blacks served as delegates to various Constitutional Conventions in the South; sixty-four as legislators; three as lieutenant governors; and four as congressmen.

Many former slaves found their mothers, fathers, sisters, brothers, children, and other loved ones sold in slavery. They worked to save money for homes and businesses. Some farmed. Others worked in trades as blacksmiths, shoemakers, bricklayers, carpenters, barbers, train porters. They were laundry women, clerks, maids, cooks. They ran businesses such as funeral homes, grocery stores, and boardinghouses. Others remained on plantations but wanted Sundays off, to receive pay for their work, and not to be whipped. They wanted their children to go to good schools to prepare for better lives. Taking new names, they asked for dignity in their new lives.

On the other hand, white people had been devastated by the War Between the States. They were angry over Lincoln freeing their property — slaves. They believed blacks were inferior and incapable of independent living. While most slaves understood their masters, most masters did not understand their slaves.

White Southerners therefore began a series of violent injustices following the war, beginning with the night riders, the Black Codes, mass murders, and lynchings. In December of 1865 in Tennessee, the Ku Klux Klan was organized and spread rapidly in the South. In other places organizations such as the Knights of the White Camellia, the Mississippi Plan, the White Brotherhood, the White League, and the Red Shirts waged practices of humiliation and intimidation of blacks through maiming and murder.

Hardworking black people were kept from saving money, dressing well, building decent homes, or advancing themselves in education. Individuals, schools, churches, and businesses that succeeded were destroyed or chased out of the South.

By 1877 President Rutherford B. Hayes decided that former slaves had had enough Northern intervention. He withdrew the troops and turned the civil rights problems over to the former slave owners, the very ones who had caused the problems. Abolitionist societies had disbanded.

Northern women, angry that black men could now vote and white women still could not, abandoned the freed people.

In 1875 the Civil Rights Act had insured African-American people the rights of all citizens. In 1883, in a reversal, the Supreme Court declared that bill unconstitutional because it aided a select group of people. Only in 1964 was that decision reversed.

This is one story in one country, but any people's story is every people's story. Injustice causes suffering everywhere. Children and adults face this question: What are we going to do about today's injustices?

Bibliography

Foner, Eric. *Reconstruction: America's Unfinished Revolution 1863–1877.* New York: Harper and Row Publishers, 1988.

Lester, Julius. *To Be a Slave.* New York: E. P. Dutton, Dial Books, 1968.

My Folks Don't Want Me to Talk About Slavery: Twenty-one Oral Histories of Former North Carolina Slaves. Edited by Belinda Hurmence. Winston-Salem, NC: John F. Blair, 1984.

Mirkin, Stanford M. *What Happened When.* New York: Ives Washburn, Inc., 1966.

The Trouble They Seen: Black People Tell the Story of Reconstruction. Edited by Dorothy Sterling. New York: Doubleday and Company, Inc., 1976.

We Are Your Sisters: Black Women in the Nineteenth Century. Edited by Dorothy Sterling. New York: W. W. Norton and Company, Inc., 1984.